"You'd love it if I just walked out of here, wouldn't you?" Alex demanded.

"Well, get used to having me around, Holly. If you'll let me have your living-room couch, I'll take that. No matter how much you protest, I'm not going away until Rico is caught."

The light in Alex's eyes told her that he meant every word of what he said. "Don't get too comfortable on that couch, Wilkins. Because you are spending one night, and one night only, there. Nothing you say will make me happy until you say goodbye." Holly was pretty sure that was the truth.

So why did it feel as if he was the cavalry riding up to rescue her? She didn't need rescuing from anything, did she? Most of her said no, but there was a sliver of common sense that told her that yes, she needed rescuing in ways that only Alex could provide.

Safe Harbor—the town where everyone finds shelter from the storm.

Books by Lynn Bulock

Love Inspired

Gifts of Grace #80
Looking for Miracles #97
Walls of Jericho #125
The Prodigal's Return #144
Change of the Heart #181
The Harbor of His Arms #204

Silhouette Romance

Surprise Package #1053
And Mommy Makes Three #1154

LYNN BULOCK

lives in Thousand Oaks, California, with her husband and two sons, a dog and a cat. She has been telling stories since she could talk and writing them down since fourth grade. She is the author of nineteen contemporary romance novels.

THE HARBOR
OF HIS ARMS

LYNN BULOCK

Published by Steeple Hill Books™

STEEPLE HILL BOOKS

Steeple Hill™

ISBN 0-373-87211-9

THE HARBOR OF HIS ARMS

Copyright © 2003 by Steeple Hill Books, Fribourg, Switzerland

Visit us at www.steeplehill.com

Printed in U.S.A.

But those who hope in the Lord
will renew their strength. They will soar on wings
like eagles; they will run and not grow weary,
they will walk and not be faint.

—*Isaiah* 40:31

To Joe, my harbor in life's storms
for over a quarter century. Here's to another
twenty-five years and more.

Chapter One

"I owe you big time for this one. Thanks again, Felicity." Holly Douglas slipped into her down jacket as she headed for the back door of The Bistro. Normally she looked forward to every hour she put in at the upscale restaurant where they both worked, but today she needed the break that Felicity's offer to cover for her provided.

Her fellow server tossed her mop of honey curls and rolled her eyes. "Oh, get a grip, Holly. I'm not giving blood or anything. Just covering the lunch shift for you on a pretty calm Wednesday. I know you'll pick up for me the next time the school calls and Jazz is sick. As usual." Holly recognized Felicity's expression. It was common to mothers of small children. They both knew that it wasn't a question of "if" the Safe Harbor Elementary would phone telling her mother that Jasmine Smith was ill. It was only a question of "when."

"Once you put it that way, it sounds better," Holly agreed. "But I can't begin to tell you how wonderful it sounds to go to this meeting today."

It was hard to put into words what the Safe Harbor Women's League meant to her. It was especially hard to tell Felicity, who was probably the only woman in town more independent than Holly. But this was the place where Holly drew the line on independence. She might not take charity from the Women's League, but the company of other understanding women was something she craved once in a while.

She looked out one of the wide windows of The Bistro. "Hope the snow holds off for a while longer. I didn't wear my boots."

"And of course you're walking over to the lighthouse." Felicity shook her head again. "Tell me you at least have a hat."

"And gloves. What do you think I am, nuts?" January in Wisconsin was not the time for foolhardy behavior.

Felicity pressed her lips together. "Okay, I'll try to stop mothering you. Make sure you're back by six, okay? Jon-Paul says it's going to be a busy night. Although how he knows this early, I have no idea.''

Holly wasn't about to argue with her boss, the owner and head chef of The Bistro. Not on what nights would be busy and which ones slack. ''He's good at predicting that. I'll be sure to get here on time.''

The light gust of wind that caught her in the parking lot made Holly's cheeks tingle. Surely it was too cold for Safe Harbor to get the snow they'd predicted this morning. At least, she was pretty sure the Green Bay radio station had said snow this far north. It was hard to hear with Conor banging drawers and Aidan howling because he couldn't find his blue toothbrush. Her boys could drown out any radio station on a good day, and this morning hadn't started off to be a good day anyway.

It was mornings like this one that she missed Kevin the most. He hadn't been home every moment when the guys were little, but when he'd been there, he'd been so good with them. Now that they were older and rowdier, it was hard not to resent the fact that she was raising them alone.

Holly tried to find a path to the lighthouse that moved her out of the way of the wind. And while she was at it she tried to put those useless thoughts of Kevin out of her mind. He was gone, and there was no changing the situation. Just like walking into the wind, she had to set her shoulders and brace for the worst.

Opening the heavy wooden door to the community meeting room at the base of the lighthouse took some effort. But the effort was worth the reward as warmth surrounded Holly in more ways than one. All over the entryway to the large, sunny room there were women chatting, shedding coats, hugging each other. Wendy Maguire must have said something interesting over in the corner where she was talking with Elizabeth Neal. The older woman burst out with a laugh and a hug for the younger Wendy.

Holly didn't have much time to contemplate what was going on in the various corners. She was a little late, as usual. There was just enough time to hang up her coat, pour a warming mug of coffee from the pot set off to one side on a long, narrow wooden table, and find a seat before the Women's League president, Constance Laughlin, got down to business.

"All right, I've let you all gossip on long enough. Who had devotions this morning?" Constance asked. Her stern-sounding words were belied by the expression in her sparkling blue eyes. Her brow wrinkled in confusion when her question brought laughter from the group. "Please, fill me in on the joke."

Elizabeth Neal was the only one brave enough to

speak. "I hate to tell you, Madame President, but last time you volunteered yourself for devotions. To kick off the year and take the burden off anyone else, I believe you said."

Constance blushed a little, covering her face with her hands. "I believe you're right. How on earth could I have forgotten that?"

"Don't be so hard on yourself, Constance. I imagine you've hardly had time to get back to normal again since the girls went back home after the holidays."

"This is true. It's really different to get a solid night's sleep again. Joey was teething the whole time Cara and David were here." Her slightly pained expression reminded Holly that she wasn't the only one with troubles. Constance's grandson Joey was named for a grandfather he would never know, since Joseph Laughlin had disappeared years before on a mission trip.

Constance had finished raising their two girls alone and had even started the Safe Harbor Women's League so that other women wouldn't have to go through the kind of pain she had alone. "It's so quiet in the house now that they're all back in Chicago again. I suppose I could say something using Psalm forty-six." There was muted laughter around the room among those who knew their Bible well enough to know that Constance was referring to a verse that admonished them all to "be still and know that I am God."

Holly found herself nodding in agreement. It wasn't often she had a moment to herself to be still even for the best of reasons, and she imagined it was the same for most of the women in the room. She was sure that managing two small kids way out on the edge of town kept Wendy Maguire busy, especially when her husband, Robert, was on call at the hospital. Annie Simmons didn't have family to tug her in different directions, but she didn't have a family to help out either, as she struggled to raise a child and at the same time open the building next door to the lighthouse as a bed-and-breakfast.

Even Elizabeth, retired as the town postmistress, didn't seem to stay still long enough for much. Every time Holly looked around she was heading some committee or other at First Peninsula Church. And that didn't begin to touch her work with the Harvest Festival every fall and the untold batches of brownies and pots of soup that seemed to pour out of her kitchen for anybody that needed them.

No, this group of women wasn't much for being still, Holly reflected. Perhaps it was why she felt so very at home here. There seemed precious little time for her to be still these days, and she despaired of knowing when there would be such a time in the future. She couldn't imagine one. Not with two active boys to raise and a life to hold together alone. It certainly wasn't what she'd planned or envisioned when she married Kevin.

He'd been in the police academy when they met, and on the force in Chicago by the time they married. So there had always been the haunting thought in the back of her mind that something could happen. Kevin always said that went with the territory. He tried to ease her fears as much as possible. In the end it hadn't done any good, because the worst had happened. Holly shook away her dire thoughts and tried to pay attention to what Constance was saying at the lectern.

She seemed to be calling for reports from the other officers of the Women's League. Wendy joined her with a large smile on her face. "I'm happy to report that all the different accounts in the treasury balance, so I'm making my final report as treasurer with a clean slate. Elizabeth, you should be able to understand all my entries and see where everything went. I even tracked down that missing $2.98 in the hospitality fund, so you won't have that plaguing you when you take office."

"Great," Elizabeth called from the front row of chairs. "Should I make a motion to accept your final report as written?"

"Please do. I have one more announcement before I end my term as treasurer." Wendy seemed to be a little flushed. "It seems that this term handling the financial records of the organization strengthened my math skills. At least in the area of addition."

Holly wondered if what Wendy was hinting about was actually true. She was saved from asking anything by Wendy volunteering the information. "It appears Robert and I are going to have another baby. According to my husband's medical expertise, there's going to be a fifth Maguire some time in July."

There were congratulations and applause around the room. Holly wondered if she was a terrible person for her strong but mixed feelings. Wendy's announcement made a wave of jealousy wash over her at the thought of the other woman, not that much older than she, who had the luxury of an intact home and a loving husband and a brand-new baby on the way. But at the same time she had to acknowledge the equally strong wave of relief that swept her, as well. Relief that it was someone else dealing with the rigors of pregnancy while also dealing with the daily life of a household and small children.

Any thought of the business meeting continuing evaporated for a while as everybody surrounded Wendy, talking about the days to come and asking her questions. So far she seemed healthy, she told them, and Robert seemed confident that she could look forward to a normal pregnancy and birth. "As normal as it gets when you're thirty-four and are chasing two little people."

"Make sure he takes some time off and gives you plenty of help," Elizabeth admonished. "Healthy or not, it won't be easy in your situation."

"I've been talking to him about that. And he may even be listening," Wendy said, her grin making the freckles spanning her cheeks dance. "Ask me in another week or two and I might have news on that front, too."

Elizabeth nodded in approval. "I hope that means that your overworked husband might actually be getting help for himself. Heaven knows it's overdue."

Constance started rapping the gavel, which no one ever paid any attention to, on the polished cherry lectern in front of her. "All right, maybe we can get back to business. Or at least let Wendy sit down and put her feet up so we don't tax her in her delicate condition."

Wendy looked as if she was threatening to stick out her tongue at Constance's suggestion. "I'm about as delicate as a plow horse, according to Robert. But I wouldn't mind sitting down for a while. Who else do we have to hear from?"

The business portion of the meeting went on for a while, and Constance got the group to stick to topic almost enough to have lunch on time. Still, it was nearly two by the time Holly was putting on her coat and getting ready to walk back to the parking lot of The Bistro to get her car and head for the grade school to pick up the boys.

That round of activity, ending with mounting the latest finger-painted treasures on the refrigerator in the apartment, took a solid hour. By three-fifteen Holly was fixing a snack for the impatient boys while they told her about their day.

They were both talking at once, sometimes finishing each other's sentences, sometimes vaulting off in totally different directions in two conversations. It never seemed to bother them. Trying to sort it all out, Holly wished she had some background with twins to help cope with her wild boys.

Aidan, slightly the taller of the two, who'd inherited more of Kevin's ruddy complexion and whose dark hair bore a distinctly reddish cast, was regaling her with things that had gone on during their outside recess after lunch. "And there were icicles hanging on the building, and Mrs. Baker said, 'Don't go over there,' so nobody did, which is good because when the sun came out one of them fell down *crash!* And it broke into about a million pieces, Mom."

"It was loud and it sparkled." Conor's observation was simpler and quieter, like Conor. Slightly shorter than his brother, and without the expansive gestures of his twin, Conor always seemed to think for a moment or two longer before he spoke. He let Aidan take the lead if anything physical needed to be done, but Holly noticed that in areas where words were needed, Aidan let Conor do the talking.

"But no one was hurt, right?" Holly was pretty sure she knew the answer, but she also knew what was important to both of her boys. They were both sensitive to the pain of others, and even the threat of anger or bloodshed disturbed them. They had been nowhere near their father's death, and too young to understand it, probably, if they had been, but still they'd absorbed something of the trauma of the adults around them. Holly felt as if she dealt every day with a little bit of that impact life had had on her boys.

"Nobody was hurt. Because we all listened to the teacher." Aidan puffed out his chest, as proud of his class and their actions as if he'd had something to do with everyone doing the right thing.

"Good," his mother said, ruffling his soft hair. "You keep listening to her, understand?"

"Okay. Can we have peanut butter on crackers?" Conor was finished with the events of the day and was ready to move on to something more important, like the state of his stomach.

Before she knew it, the boy's favorite baby-sitter was at the door and Holly needed to finish getting ready for work.

She gave Brett the instructions he needed and kissed the boys goodbye. It did her heart good to see that they barely noticed she was leaving.

Even in the snow that had started to fall it didn't take long to get from the apartment complex to The Bistro. Holly could see that Jon-Paul had been right in his predictions. It was still a little before six, and there were already a good number of cars in the lot.

"All right! Even five minutes early," Felicity crowed. "This is a pleasant surprise."

Holly scrunched up her nose. "I'm not that predictably late, am I? Don't answer that." The grin on Felicity's face answered for her.

They went over the evening's specials together and Jon-Paul filled her in on the few changes he'd made during preparation of the night's featured dishes. Felicity's hand was on the swinging door between the kitchen and the dining room when she turned back to look at Holly. "I almost forgot—you already have one customer. A fairly good-looking younger guy came in alone and asked specifically for one of your tables. He said he'd wait for you no matter when you showed up."

"That's odd. I can't imagine who that would be."

"No old flames or anything?"

"Not a clue." Holly couldn't even think of anybody who knew she was in Safe Harbor, Wisconsin, who fit Felicity's description. A growing dread told her that anyone looking for her here couldn't mean good things. She tried to push the feeling away and listen to what Felicity was saying about the stranger.

"He asked for coffee, and I've refilled it once. But otherwise he said he'd wait for you." Felicity went out to check on her own tables, and Holly got ready for her mystery customer and the rest of the evening rush. She looked at the specials board again, trying to commit everything to memory.

The swinging door whooshed behind her as she entered the dining room. The inside of The Bistro looked like the perfect place to be on a wintry night like this. The fire in the big brick fireplace cast a cozy glow on the big dining room. Surely no place this welcoming and cozy could hold danger.

At the corner table in "her" section, a man sat with his back to her, and his back to the fire. Holly didn't recognize him right away from his back view, with his neatly cut sandy-brown hair and nondescript jacket.

"Hi, welcome to The Bistro. My name is Holly and I'll be your server this evening. Would you like to hear our specials?" She got the whole spiel out before she made eye contact with the stranger and her world collapsed in a split second.

Chapter Two

"You don't look glad to see me." Alex Wilkins figured that was the understatement of the century. Holly Douglas looked horrified. She had barely kept from dropping the leatherette case holding her order pad, and the pen she had grasped in her other hand slid to the floor.

He almost wished her dark hair hadn't been swept back away from her face. Maybe if she'd had the luxury of letting it cover her flushed cheeks she could have pretended to be more glad to see him. Even that was doubtful.

Sitting in the cushy booth in this romantic restaurant, reducing a woman to tears by his very presence, Alex decided he definitely hated his job. Nobody was ever glad to see him. It was like being a dentist who only did root canals. No, they all knew it was bad news or an arrest warrant when he was there. Even his own superiors weren't that happy to see him most days. Since as one of their lead investigators they handed him only the complicated stuff, they were usually in foul moods even before he got to them.

"You're right. I'm not glad to see you." Holly's soft voice, choked with emotion, broke into his thoughts. "This can't be a social call. Nobody drives over sixty miles in January just to visit in this neck of the woods."

"Sounds like you're fitting in with the locals real well. Wish I could tell you that a social call was all I was here for. I'd love to be able to say I made this drive just to check up on you." Alex watched her face while he spoke to her.

The woman might have been married to a cop, but she hadn't picked up a cop's habits. She still wore her emotions for all to see. Including that flutter of hope when she thought for a split second that seeing him didn't mean more bad news.

"Of course you didn't. That would make my life too easy. And life right now is never easy." Holly snapped open that order pad again. "But you better be on the county's expense account, because I can't stand here and chat all night with somebody who's not ordering dinner."

"Steak. Medium rare. With a baked potato—none of that trendy garlic-mashed, goat cheese stuff." That got the first ghost of a smile out of her he'd seen. "And a salad, if it's going to be made up of things I can recognize."

"For you, I'll have Jon-Paul put together his famous NWS special."

"Okay, you have me interested. What's that?"

This time the smile flashed into an honest grin, and Alex was reminded that Holly Douglas was a young woman, not even thirty. Only the care and trouble of the past few years had dimmed the natural beauty in the planes of her face. "The No Weed Salad. A nice chunk of iceberg flat on a plate with Thousand Island dressing."

"Make it blue cheese and you have a deal."

"Will do. And Alex? I have plenty to do for the next three hours. So don't expect any more attention than the rest of my customers."

"Don't worry. I'm a good tipper, even when the county isn't paying. And things are mostly okay, Holly. I just have a little news you're not going to want to hear. It will keep until you get done with your shift."

She looked visibly relieved. Alex felt bad for a split second for trivializing what he'd been sent here to tell her. Holly wouldn't look that happy again for quite some time once she heard what he had to say.

Still, there was no sense upsetting her when she had work to do. Having another three hours of blissful ignorance of the latest happenings in Cook County, Illinois, wouldn't change Holly's life in the long run. And it would give Alex a little more time to figure out how to break the news that this new life they'd set up for her might all be tumbling down.

While he thought about what he was going to say, Alex scanned the large room that made up the main dining area of The Bistro. He wondered how Holly went to work here every day. The place was designed for couples to sit at the tufted leather booths, leaning over flickering candlelight. At some of the larger tables there were family groups, or bunches of friends, all of whom would have reminded him on a daily basis of what he was missing as a single adult. And Holly wasn't single by choice.

Kevin Douglas should still be doing his job on the force, coming home at night to his pretty wife and active kids. They had twins, didn't they? It was what Alex remembered, and he struggled to recall how old the boys would be now. Old enough to realize that their daddy wasn't coming back, that was for sure. And old enough to realize something was up when he came home with their mother tonight. Alex hoped they'd be tucked into bed before he went home with Holly. That way there would be one less scene in the course of the evening.

"Tell Jon-Paul that his salad was superb. Almost as good as his steak," Alex said two hours later as he stretched his legs out under the table.

"I will. Does all this praise mean you don't have any room for a piece of apple pie?"

"Nobody ever said that. Think you could swing a scoop of ice cream on top, too?"

"Sure. We even have homemade cinnamon ice cream. I know it's not the traditional vanilla, but you have to let Jon-Paul have his flourish someplace, don't you? He gets cranky if all his artful touches are denied."

"Cinnamon ice cream I can handle. Especially after he went to all the trouble to make the rest of the meal as fuss free as possible."

"Coffee? For most folks I'd suggest decaf this late at night, but I don't suppose you're interested."

"High-test or nothing," Alex informed her. "And yes, I'd take a cup. Please." His manners were awful. Maybe he just wasn't used to dining anywhere as pleasant as The Bistro. He'd better get used to it, he thought. It was probably going to be his home away from home for a few days, or maybe even weeks.

Holly came back with the pie and coffee, setting them down in front of him. "Okay, the worst of the rush is over. I need to know what this visit is all about."

His heart sank. She looked so happy. But he couldn't put his news off much longer. It would be nice to try, though. "How about I tell you at home?"

Her look went from serious to stern. "I don't remember inviting you home with me."

Here it went. There was no putting things off any longer. "When I'm done talking, I'll be inviting myself home if you don't do it. Our friend Rico Salazar is out on the street. A combination of a good lawyer and a bad ruling. By the time we could convince the judge that he really, really shouldn't be released no matter what the bail, he'd slipped through our fingers."

He watched Holly's face pale to the color of the walls around him at the knowledge that her husband's killer was free. Lower lip trembling, she fled, leaving him to contemplate his melting ice cream and cooling coffee. His appetite for either wasn't very high right now.

Before he could decide what to do, the young woman who had seated him when he came in was standing before him, and she looked very angry. "All right, what did you say to her? Holly's crying. And Holly never cries. Even the night when we got the whole table of jerks from Milwaukee, who had too much to drink, Holly didn't cry. Not even when Jon-Paul threw them all out personally after they said those mean things to her. So what did you do?'' His accuser waved a long finger in his face, curls bouncing around her glowing face. What could he tell this baby virago?

She wasn't going to take silence as an answer. Wild curls still bouncing, foot tapping in impatience, she stayed planted right in front of him. ''Well? You looked okay, and I was glad to see somebody that Holly knew for a change, but I'm beginning to change my mind. Should I have Jon-Paul out here? He played pro ball for a little while before he opened the restaurant. Does all the bouncer work around here himself.'' She narrowed her eyes in determination, and Alex knew he had to talk fast.

''No, really, things aren't that bad. I had to give Holly a bit of bad news. But I'm on her side, honest.''

''It sure didn't look that way when she came back in the kitchen just now.'' This young woman still needed some convincing. ''She looked upset. And like I said before, she never gets that upset over anything.''

''Felicity? Are you looking out for me?'' A trembly voice came from behind Alex's tormentor. ''That is so sweet, but really I'm okay. And Alex is all right. Just barely, but it isn't his fault that I'm acting like this.'' Felicity turned toward Holly and put her hands on Holly's shoulders.

"You sure? Because we can have Jon-Paul take care of him." Her tone of voice told Alex it would be no trouble, either. He made a mental note to stay on this young woman's good side whenever possible.

"I'm sure. And he's more dangerous than he looks, Felicity. But at least he's one of the good guys. He used to work with my husband, and he's here to look after me."

Alex was surprised to hear Holly admit to that much. He was pretty sure that nobody in this little Wisconsin town knew much about Holly's past. With every word she spoke she looked more composed. She used one slender hand to push an escaped lock of her dark hair away from her face, and perhaps remove the last traces of tears from her cheek. "Besides, Alex won't be a problem for much longer. I'm back out here to thank him for his concern and send him back to Chicago where he belongs."

So that was what she was up to. Well, Holly Douglas had more than one surprise coming tonight. "I'm afraid that's not possible, Holly. But maybe we can discuss it in a less public environment. We'll have the time, because I'm not leaving town before our mutual friend is back in police custody."

Alex didn't know which expression he liked least on the lovely faces in front of him. From his limited experience he would have said Felicity would be more trouble in the short run, with her amazement and anger blending. However, he'd known Holly quite a bit longer, and so knew her a little bit better. And he knew just enough to tell that in the long run, the look of determination narrowing her eyes and drawing tight lines in her face was going to mean much more trouble for him.

It was going to be a long night. He prayed it wasn't going to be the first of quite a few. Maybe luck would be on his side for a change and they'd have Rico back in the fold soon. Right. And maybe they'd solve all the world's problems while they were at it and he could get a great job teaching third grade because nobody would need the services of a cop with a law degree anymore.

Meanwhile he was stuck here in Safe Harbor, Wisconsin, with a woman who didn't want to be looked after, a cold cup of coffee and a slice of apple pie floating in melted ice cream. As he'd said before, it was going to be a long night.

So what could she do with this guy? Holly paced the kitchen of The Bistro, trying to decide how to gather her thoughts, and what to tell her boss and Felicity. They had both been so kind to her for all these months. They deserved some kind of explanation for her behavior. They also deserved some more information about what the slightly menacing-looking stranger was doing in the dining room. She hadn't thought of Alex Wilkins in a long while before tonight, and had never looked at him with the eyes of a stranger.

For her he'd always been Kevin's friend on the force, first in his role as an undercover officer, then later as an investigator with the district attorney's office. Sure, he'd looked a little rough around the edges. But most of Kevin's friends and co-workers had looked that way. Kevin had called the drug enforcement officers that he'd mostly dealt with "the wolf pack," and it had been an apt name. They had a lean, ragged look about them that seemed to suggest they were on the fringes of society and liked things that way just fine. Kevin had always stuck out with his boyish Irish good looks, earning him the nickname of "The Choirboy" and getting him some desperately dangerous assignments just because nobody suspected him.

He'd loved every minute of it, she knew that. And from what Alex and others had told her, what they could tell her after Kevin's death, he'd been very good at what he did. Why couldn't those who followed after him have been as good at what they did so scum like Rico stayed in custody? It certainly would make her life easier. Or at least she would have been without this latest complication. Nothing was particularly easy about life right now. Raising two active little boys with no father, and limited income, put a daily strain on Holly's patience and her bank account. Now to add looking over her shoulder again was the last thing she needed.

Jon-Paul walked away from the range where he was supervising a sous-chef with half a dozen sauté pans going and stood in front of Holly. "Okay, you ready to talk? Felicity says that guy out there made you cry. Is she right?"

Holly managed what she knew was a wan smile for her overprotective boss. "Not exactly. He didn't make me cry the way she thinks he did. I'll admit I was crying, but it wasn't exactly Alex's fault. He's just an old friend of my husband's, and he had a little bad news for me. Nothing I can't handle. And nothing you need to get involved in."

"You sure?" There were times when Holly thought that Jon-Paul missed the action he'd gotten playing football. He certainly didn't seem to shy away from confrontation.

"Positive. But thanks for caring."

His scowl lightened into a grin. "Hey, you're my best server. I can't have you upset." He looked around the kitchen at the chefs and assistants who were finishing up the last of the late dinner orders. "Why don't you take off a little early and take care of your business with your friend."

"Sounds like a good idea. You sure you don't mind?" Holly minded a little herself, just because taking off early meant less income in tips. But the dining crowd was thinning, and there wouldn't be that much more income to be had anyway. Alex's presence would have her so rattled that she wouldn't be that effective to begin with. As usual, Jon-Paul had a good idea.

"I'm positive. See you for lunch tomorrow, right?"

"Bright and early." Holly tried to sound more cheerful about the prospect than she felt. She went back to the dining room to try to make Alex see things from her perspective. It wasn't a likely prospect, but she was sure going to try.

She knew she was going to lose the argument when he wouldn't even consider her offer of dinner on the house. "No, I'm going to be here a while," he argued, ignoring her pointed looks that tried to tell him otherwise. "No sense in getting off on the wrong foot. I intend to start out as a paying customer and stay that way. Besides, the one perk to being with the D.A.'s office is that I do have an expense account. It might not be the world's most liberal one, but it will suit my needs well in a little town like this in Wisconsin."

"If you insist." Holly tried to sound as pleasant as possible. It wasn't easy. She hated losing arguments. And lately it seemed as if she got in more arguments every day, and seldom won one. This one had all the earmarks of being a major defeat already.

"And I do insist. I insist on paying for my dinner, and I insist on staying here in town. The closer I can stay to you, the better."

"Well, that might present a little problem, because Safe Harbor isn't the kind of place where a woman in my situation can just take in a guy off the street without a lot of talk."

"So tell them the truth." Alex could be just as argumentative as she was. "Tell them I'm your bodyguard because of the situation Kevin left you in."

"He didn't leave me in any situation," she fired back. "And I can't tell them the rest of the truth, anyway."

"Why not? Surely it would be better than having your fine, upstanding small-town friends think you were taking in strays."

"It really isn't any of your business what my friends will think. And surely that expense account will spring for a hotel room if we can find one. Your timing is at least a month off. If you could have held off until after Valentine's Day I could have got you a room at the new bed-and-breakfast."

"Sorry the bad guys weren't paying attention to your social calendar."

"Oh, stow it, Wilkins. I know you're sorry about

a lot of things, but I'm sure that isn't one of them.''
Holly knew she sounded unkind, but she felt unkind
right now, and anxious to get rid of Alex Wilkins
and the problems he posed.

He wasn't cooperating. Alex sat still, folding his
arms over his chest. ''You'd love it if I just walked
out of here, wouldn't you? Well, get used to having
me around, because no matter how much you protest, or how many reasons you have to the contrary,
I'm staying. And for tonight I'm camping out as
close to you as I can get. If you'll let me have your
living-room couch, I'll take that. Otherwise I'll sleep
in my car in the apartment-complex parking lot. But
I'm not going away, Holly.''

The light in his eyes told her he meant every word
of what he said. That was a shame, because now
Holly was stuck. She had no desire to let Alex Wilkins into her apartment for any reason. But only a
heartless monster would let anybody sleep in a car
in January this far north. Of course Alex knew that.
It was why he'd played that trump card to begin
with.

''Don't get comfortable on that couch, Wilkins.
Because you're spending one night, and one night
only, there. And you can be the one to come up with
an explanation for my boys about who you are and
why you're on that couch. Remember they're only
five.''

Alex looked thoughtful while he took a credit

card out of his pocket to settle his bill. "Now you make sleeping in the car sound attractive." He'd lost that challenging grin. "If I thought I wouldn't freeze to death I'd stay there. Five years old, huh? I'll have to dredge back in the distant past and try to remember what I thought about when I was five. Maybe I can come up with something convincing that will satisfy them and make you happy at the same time."

Holly picked up the credit card and headed toward the kitchen. "Don't bet on it. You might convince the boys, but nothing you say will make me happy until you say goodbye." She was pretty sure that was the truth. Why didn't it feel much like the truth when she said it?

Holly puzzled the question over in her mind while she got Alex's receipt and prepared to give him directions to her apartment. Surely any sane, respectable person would be glad to have someone like Alex out of her life as quickly as possible.

Why, instead, did it seem as if he was the cavalry riding up to rescue her? She didn't need rescuing from anything, did she? Most of her said no, but there was a sliver of common sense that told her yes, she needed rescuing in ways that Alex could probably provide. It was only a few blocks back to the apartment, not nearly enough time to answer a question that complex, so Holly wasn't surprised when she pulled up in the parking lot with no more answers than she'd had at The Bistro.

Chapter Three

Alex had to admire Holly's baby-sitter. The kid looked only about fifteen or sixteen, but he seemed very protective of her. This was obviously the first time Holly had ever come home from work earlier than planned, or brought company with her, and the boy eyed Alex suspiciously.

Neither of the rowdy little boys the teenager had been watching appeared to like the idea of a strange man coming home with Mom, either. Holly paid the sitter, and Alex could hear her reassuring him at the doorway that everything was okay. While that was going on, he sat down on the lumpy brown couch in the living room. The little boys stared at him in silence.

"Who are you, anyway?" One of them broke his

silence and stepped half a pace closer to Alex. There was still a coffee table between them to keep the kid brave. Alex could see a bit of Kevin Douglas in this one. His brown hair looked as if it had a mind of its own, and his challenging posture made him seem much taller than he was.

"I'm a friend of your dad's. My name is Alex Wilkins."

"Okay." The answer didn't seem to satisfy the child totally. "I'm Conor. This is Aidan." He motioned toward his silent brother, who was slightly taller.

Alex could hear the baby-sitter ask a question, and then Holly closed the door behind him. Alex was happy to see that she locked it securely. "So you've introduced yourself?"

"I have. Just the basics. I told them my name, and that I was a friend of their dad's. Anything else I should add?"

"Only that you won't be here long, and that it's still time for bed, whether we have company or not," Holly said firmly. Conor seemed about to protest, but one look at his mother made him think better of it. If he'd gotten that look from a woman, Alex thought, he wouldn't argue, either. Holly started hustling the two boys toward the hall.

While she was putting the boys to bed, Alex took in his surroundings. Everything was as neat as he'd expect a home with two five-year-olds to be, and under the clutter it was all very clean. Other than the boys' toys and the basics, there wasn't much to see.

Holly's couch wasn't the most comfortable thing Alex had ever thought about sleeping on. It beat sitting straight up in a car seat, or slouched over in one doing a stakeout, but that was about the nicest thing he could say about it. The couch was far from new, and there had obviously been a lot of kid feet bouncing on it over the years. That would account for the sagging springs, anyway.

The room was warmer than his car would have been, and it was quiet enough. Once Holly had put the kids to bed she came out of their room quietly. She went to a linen closet, got supplies, handed him a pillow and blanket and pointed out the remote for the television. "If you turn on the TV, keep it quiet. Conor's a light sleeper. Aidan would sleep through a hurricane, but his brother hears mouse footsteps, I swear."

"I'll keep it low," he promised. Holly went to bed at that point. Without another word she disappeared into the other bedroom, and Alex didn't see her again. He wondered what kinds of thoughts were rolling through her mind.

He knew what was going through his. How could

he do his job, help Holly without messing up her life, and get out of this town as quickly as possible?

In the morning he could feel someone watching him before he opened his eyes. The instinct to react was so strong that he thanked God for the foresight he'd had in locking up his automatic in the gun safe built into his car trunk.

He opened his eyes to see a short, freckle-faced figure standing in front of him, regarding him seriously. Without seeing both twins, he wondered who he was looking at. "Good morning," he said, wondering if a kid this young knew where his mom kept the coffee. He was definitely going to have to find out.

"Hi. I'm Conor," the boy said, ending Alex's confusion over that point, at least. "What's your name again?"

"Alex. Alex Wilkins."

"Oh, yeah. You said you were a friend of my dad's, right?"

"Right."

Conor seemed to think about that. "From before or from now?"

That had him stumped. "From before, I think. What do you mean?"

The kid wrinkled his brow. "Well, Mom says Dad's in heaven with Jesus and the angels now, and you're sure not Jesus and you don't look like any angel.''

Alex didn't know whether to laugh or be stunned by the depth of the kid's thoughts. "Trust me, I'm not an angel."

"I didn't think so. That's too bad. We could sure use one."

This was interesting. Maybe Holly wasn't as independent and "okay" as she had portrayed herself. "Oh, yeah?"

Conor apparently trusted him enough to sit down on the edge of the couch next to him. "Yeah. Mom's always talking to God and Dad when she thinks we don't hear her. And she's sure asking them for help a lot lately.''

Alex felt a lump in his throat. How did he answer this? "Well, like I said, I'm not an angel. But maybe I can help out some while I'm here. For right now, *you* could help *me* out."

"Me? How?" Conor didn't look as if he believed that for a moment.

"You could go into the kitchen with me and show me where your mom keeps the coffee. Who knows, maybe I could even fix breakfast for both of us while I'm there."

"I'll try. But I think we're out of coffee. And I think we're out of the right kind of cereal, too. I think that's why Mom was talking to God and Dad so loud yesterday while she was getting ready for work.''

Great. Alex hadn't talked to this kid for ten minutes yet and already he knew a lot more about Holly's personal life than he cared to know. "Well, maybe we can do something about that. Let's go out in the kitchen and look anyway, okay?''

"Okay. But don't make any noise. I'm not supposed to make any noise until Mom's alarm goes off. And no touching anything glass, or knives, or opening the refrigerator....''

"I get the picture, Conor." If Holly was really out of coffee, he might have to break a few rules around here before the lady of the house even got out of bed.

Walking into the kitchen and having Conor show him around made Alex wary somehow. The space reminded him of something, brought a memory from his past almost to the surface. Whatever it was lay just beneath where Alex could access it as he searched the clean, bare countertops and looked briefly in the cabinets.

"Well, you're right, Conor," he said after his foray. "There is no coffee here, not even in the freezer. And unless the right kind of cereal is plain corn flakes, it isn't here, either.''

Conor made a noise of disgust. "Corn flakes. Nobody but Mom likes corn flakes. And we all had them for breakfast yesterday. There weren't even any bananas.'' He wrinkled his nose and sat down on one of the worn kitchen chairs. "Mom said she was going to the grocery store after work last night. I bet she forgot.''

"If she did, it's because of me. I kind of came in where she works and surprised her.'' He sat down at one of the other chairs, sliding it out quietly to keep to Conor's "no noise'' rules. If he hadn't woken Holly or Conor's twin brother already, maybe he'd get lucky and let them sleep a while longer.

"I hope it was a good surprise.'' Conor seemed to be accusing him of something. The serious look on the child's face and his crossed arms brought Alex's memory to the surface. It wasn't a pleasant one, and he wished that he'd been able to leave it buried.

This was a replica of his kitchen when he was a kid, or at least one of them. His dad's navy career had put them through at least a dozen kitchens by the time Alex had left home at sixteen.

It wasn't the look of this kitchen that reminded him of his mother's kitchens, but more the feel of it. Everything was spare and stark, clean but some-what empty. The very basics were there, but very little else. No cute little canisters held tea and home-made cookies. Other than the kid art on the refrigerator gallery, there wasn't much that added color to the room.

Alex wondered if there was a reason Holly's kitchen reminded him of those his mother had tried to make into homes twenty years ago. He hoped there was little cause at all, other than the similarity of two harried mothers raising kids virtually alone under tight circumstances.

Conor definitely had the serious air he'd had as a child, protective of his mother. Alex had never felt as if he'd protected his own mother enough, even though he'd been a child at the time. But this mother he could help in several ways. "Come on, Conor," he told his companion. "We're going to make a breakfast run."

Holly's alarm beeped insistently, and she groped for it. Just ten more minutes of sleep would feel so good. Her eyes opened as her fingers hit the button, and in an instant she was sitting straight up, feet over the edge of the bed, ready to spring into action. It was much too light out for this to be her normal time to get up. She must have hit the snooze alarm without knowing it, maybe even several times already.

She could hear voices in the kitchen. At first hearing three voices, one of them a deep adult male, disoriented her. Then she remembered last night and all its surprises. Alex was in her kitchen with the boys. Knowing that was enough to get her up and out of bed all the way in a hurry. She pulled on sweatpants to go with the T-shirt she'd slept in and raced out to the kitchen, oblivious to what she must look like.

Holly wasn't sure what she had expected in the kitchen, but she certainly hadn't anticipated the breakfast party she found. "Hi, Mom." Aidan backhanded a suspiciously dark milk mustache, grinning. "Alex got doughnuts. The good kind with sprinkles. And chocolate milk, but only a little bit."

"What happened here?" Holly didn't know whether to be stunned or gratified that Alex had gotten the kids breakfast. It wasn't what she would have allowed them to have, but they'd have to deal with that issue later. There wasn't any sense in forbidding doughnuts that had already been eaten.

Alex shrugged, sipping coffee out of a mug. "Just breakfast. Conor was up early and he informed me that you were out of coffee, so we made a quick run down the street to solve that problem. The closest place we could find to get breakfast stuff was the bakery. And I'm a sucker for doughnuts with sprinkles, too." His smile was disarming.

Holly sat down, unsure where to begin the questions she had. "How did you get there? Conor and Aidan both have booster seats for the car. I'll bet you let him ride up front without a seat, didn't you?'' She was amazed at how angry the thought made her.

"Not a chance. I may not have kids, but I know that much about safety. He rode in the back, in his own booster seat. You left your car unlocked last night when we got here, apparently.'' His warning look told Holly that he wanted to discuss that subject later.

His accusation made her defensive. "Have you really looked at that car? Who would steal a twelve-year-old sedan with that kind of rust damage?''

"Nobody, especially in a little town like this. But that wasn't what I was talking about, and you know it." Alex didn't say any more, just lifted his coffee to his lips. "I got you a coffee, too, by the way. And Aidan's right—I only got one container of chocolate milk. The gallon I bought was regular one percent. I figured I had to do something to earn points with you.''

"Thank you.'' Holly got up and went toward the kitchen countertop. She wasn't sure what she was thanking Alex for the most—getting breakfast for everyone when she didn't have the energy, giving the boys a much-needed treat that she could not have provided or not mentioning her safety in front of her children.

"You're welcome." His quiet answer made Holly

shiver. It was as if he'd understood all three of her reasons for thanking him. She wasn't used to having another adult to talk to most of the time. Especially not a man, and definitely not one who understood her. She had figured she'd lost that luxury for good when Kevin died.

She hid her confusion by grabbing her cardboard cup of coffee. Opening the cabinet, she got a mug out and poured the coffee in. She took a moment to bring it up to full steam in the microwave and sat down at the table with the mug, hoping she could mask the whirl of feelings that threatened to swamp her.

"We saved you one, Mom." Aidan pushed the box closer to her, coming perilously close to knocking over her coffee. A veteran of such encounters, Holly moved her mug in time.

"Good for you. And it's even the cinnamon kind. Who told Mr. Wilkins that I liked those?"

It was Conor's turn to grin this time. "I did. And he said to call him Alex, Mom, not Mr. Wilkins. Is that okay?"

"If that's what he said, Conor." She looked around the table at the crumbs and mostly empty milk glasses. "Now, if you guys are done with breakfast, how about going in and washing your hands and faces again and getting dressed for school?"

Aidan took one last swig of chocolate milk and the two of them were off. "I didn't think about that much sugar in them on a school morning," Alex said. "Hope their teacher doesn't threaten to strangle me."

"Don't worry, they'll burn it off before they get there. Fortunately sugar isn't a problem for either of them." Holly looked at her overnight guest. He didn't really look as if he'd slept a lot better than she had. His hair was still a bit rumpled, and the flannel shirt he was wearing had the earmarks of having been slept in. "So, what did they ask you? And what did you tell them?"

Alex sighed and ran a hand through his sandy hair. "Conor's sharp for five. I'll bet you have a challenge keeping up with him."

"I do. He's always the one with the questions I can't answer. Aidan is satisfied with a lot less in the way of explanations."

"Yeah, knowing that I was an old work buddy of Kevin's was enough for him. That and doughnuts." Alex grinned out of one side of his mouth.

"The chocolate milk didn't hurt, either. Smart move, Wilkins."

The grin made it all the way to his tired eyes this time. "Guys and food bribery. It does solve a lot of problems."

"True. But it won't solve all the problems this

time. We're going to need to figure out something to tell them without going into the details about Rico. They know very little about Kevin's death, and I intend to keep it that way until they're a lot older.''

''And they're much too young to have to deal with this situation,'' Alex agreed. ''Conor did mention that maybe you could use a little help around here. Maybe we could just leave things at that. Tell them that I've come to help out for a while.''

''We don't need that much help.'' Holly knew she sounded argumentative, but it was the way she felt. ''I can take care of my kids and myself just fine, thank you.''

''I know you can. But you shouldn't have to. Especially not in this situation, Holly.'' His hand slid over the table to cover hers. ''I know this has to be rough. How rough I can't even imagine as a single guy with no one depending on me. Now Cook County has added to your burden by messing up Rico's custody arrangements. At least let me try to make that up to you.''

Holly drew her hand out from under his. It felt too good to have that human contact, and she surely couldn't get used to it. ''There's no way you can make up to me what Cook County did to mess up my life. But I know you're not going away for a while, so I might as well get used to you.'' She'd try to get used to him, anyway. It would be difficult to do without depending on him, but Holly knew that she couldn't depend on anybody anymore. The past eighteen months had certainly taught her that. "What do I owe you for breakfast?"

He waved away her concern before she could reach for her purse. "Nothing. I spent less altogether than I would have for one coffee and a scone in Chicago."

"Well, don't make a habit of providing the groceries around here."

"Only as long as I'm eating part of them. Will we have time for a supermarket run once you drop these guys off at school? I only got one cup of coffee for each of us, and I can guarantee that I'll be looking for more before we go in to The Bistro later."

Holly felt tired already. Having Alex around was certainly going to complicate her life. Maybe if she didn't argue with him, and showed him enough of what her normal life was like, he'd lose interest quickly. "Sure. Now, why don't you go break up the water fight that I know is going on in the bathroom so that we can get those guys to school on time and relatively dry?"

It surprised her to see that he seemed to relish the prospect. "Will do. They need any help with getting dressed or anything while I'm in there?"

Holly tried not to smirk. "Try asking them that and see the answer you get." The ruckus that would follow that kind of question would be worth the price of admission. Maybe having Alex around wouldn't last long after all. Surely a day or two of this would have him hightailing it back to Chicago.

He rose, grinning. "I don't think so. You look like that would be too easy. And I have to remember they're independent guys even if they aren't very tall. Even at five, I don't remember wanting help with much of anything. I'll settle for breaking up the water fight. And once we get them dropped off, you and I are going to have a long conversation on personal safety."

He was going to be a hard one to shake, Holly thought as he retreated to the hall bathroom. Something about watching him from a rear view made her worry about more than just getting rid of him. Seeing him in jeans early in the morning, Holly could tell that having Alex around was going to be more threatening to her personal safety than worrying about Rico out there someplace in the shadows.

Chapter Four

Grocery shopping with Alex was a nerve-racking experience for Holly. She was sure she would rather have been pushing the cart through the aisles with both boys along, and that was her least favorite way to shop. But Alex was much more adamant about putting into the cart large numbers of things she couldn't afford and didn't usually get. And unlike her boys, a pointed look in his direction did not make him put things back on the shelves.

In fact, no amount of arguing made him stick to her list or her budget. "You're not doing me any favors in the long run," she told him when he put the third expensive package of meat into the cart. "Once you're gone in a few days the boys will only wonder why I'm not getting all this again."

"Then they'll be happy to have good old Uncle Alex stick around a while, won't they?"

It was all Holly could do not to roll her eyes. "That's what they'll see when they look at you, isn't it? An uncle to spoil them and let them do things that I wouldn't on a bet. Of course they'll be happy to keep you around."

"Hey, I'd think you'd be just as happy. You get a little help, and Cook County pays both at the same time. If I were in your shoes it wouldn't bother me to have them pay for a whole lot."

Holly didn't know how to answer that one. She'd tried hard not to blame the police force for Kevin's death. It had been a struggle not to blame his job, or God, or even fate or whatever for what had happened. None of those alternatives seemed like the Christian way to deal with what had happened. But if she were honest with herself, the kind of feelings Alex was describing welled up in her more often than she'd like to admit. How did he do that? She didn't remember inviting Alex Wilkins into her personal world of thoughts and feelings, yet he managed to get there often enough to make her quite uncomfortable.

She hoped her discomfort didn't show. Holly wasn't ready to share her deepest feelings with this man yet. "Well, be glad you're not in my shoes. Because it's not a very nice place to be right now."

Even that amount of honesty surprised her. She was used to keeping her problems to herself. What was it about squabbling over expensive cookies in the grocery store with this man that brought out so many mixed feelings?

"Gee, do I sense a little hostility here?" Alex stepped back from the cart. "If so, hooray. You need to vent some of that once in a while, Holly."

She pushed the half-loaded basket past him, narrowly missing his toes. He was a cool customer; he didn't even flinch when the cart rolled by that close. "Since when have you added psychologist to your other degrees, Wilkins? It doesn't become you."

"Not really psychology, just common sense. There's still plenty of that taught in the academy and at law school. Maybe even we don't apply it as often as we should."

"How's that?" He sounded genuinely concerned, and Holly wanted to know what he meant.

"I've been telling the brass for years that we don't give enough support to victims and their families. Which is why I probably got this assignment," he finished with a rueful grin. "Maybe they figure if I see what that kind of support actually entails I won't be so quick to volunteer it."

"Suits me. Then maybe I can get back to life as I know it." Holly pushed the cart past another aisle, anxious to get out of the store without too much more goody-buying from Alex.

He wasn't about to let her get away easily. Alex walked in front and put both hands on the end of the cart, blocking her way. "Yeah, well, don't be so quick to go back to life as you know it. You weren't doing that great a job, Holly."

His gaze on her made a shiver run up her spine. She couldn't ignore the serious tone of what he said or the implications of the words, either. "What— what do you mean by that?" she stammered.

"I may have only been here a day or so, but I've looked around. In a perfectly normal situation you'd be doing an okay job. But this isn't a perfectly normal situation. And from what I've seen, you're stressed and short on patience and money. Raising kids alone can't be fun or easy."

"No, but it's reality, so you might as well let me get back to it." Holly felt like folding her arms and pouting. Of course, neither action would make Alex take her any more seriously.

"Sorry, I can't do that. I think I've made it perfectly clear that I'm not leaving for a while. I want to make sure you're plenty safe first. You and the boys."

"We'll be safe. We have been for the entire time we've lived in Safe Harbor. It's well named," Holly argued.

"Not good enough. You were safe then because Rico was behind bars. Now he's not, and that changes things. Besides, remember what I said earlier? That I was able to take Conor with me in his own car seat because none of the car doors were locked? You can't be that lax, even after I go back to Chicago. Rico has friends. And they have friends. This may not be over for years."

"Great. Just what I wanted to hear."

He still wasn't letting the basket move. "Whether you want to hear what I have to say or not, you have to listen. And listening means doing what I'm asking, like locking the car doors. Can we agree on that?"

Her aggravation and anxiety levels were growing by the second. Wasn't there anything she could say that would make him listen? This was her life they were talking about, and she wanted to stay in control. "But Alex, I'll stick out like a sore thumb. Nobody in Safe Harbor is that concerned about security. It's a very small town."

Shaking his head, Alex finally let go of the cart. He wasn't letting go of his ideas, though. "Yeah, it's a small town, all right. With a very small police force, I'll bet. And a large tourist population."

"So?"

"So nobody would notice a stranger like Rico or the guys he hangs out with if they came around looking for you. The Safe Harbor force has gotten our bulletins, but they don't know how you fit in. The force here will have to be educated on what to look for, and chances are nobody around here is ready. Maybe I can make some money while I'm here, giving security seminars. Reimburse the county for some of these expensive groceries." He illustrated his point by putting two half gallons of ice cream into the cart. It wasn't the store brand, either.

Holly gave up. Arguing with him only made him more determined. "All right. Fine. I'll lock the car doors. And make sure the dead bolt is on at night in the apartment."

"And screen your phone calls. You do have caller ID, don't you?"

The man was relentless. "Sure. Whatever." Whatever was going to get him out of her hair the fastest. And if that meant agreeing with him on all his much-too-cautious safety notions, so be it. They were coming up to the checkout counter now and she knew there wasn't enough money in her purse to pay for this heaped cart of food. So arguing with Alex at this point would be counterproductive.

But then, Holly was beginning to get the idea that arguing with Alex at any point was going to be fairly useless. He was a man used to getting his way. She might have plenty of experience arguing with stub-

born little boys, but Alex with his courtroom training was a whole different kind of adversary.

Didn't the woman ever get tired of arguing? Alex
picked up as many plastic sacks of groceries as he
was sure he could take in one load and straightened
up from the car trunk. If he took any less she'd only
load herself down, sure that she needed to pull her
weight in every endeavor. He wasn't sure if he'd
ever met anybody this stubborn. His aggravation
probably made him close the trunk a little more
forcefully than he should, but he had to get rid of
some frustrations somewhere.

Independence was a wonderful thing, especially
in a situation like the one Holly found herself in.
When she didn't have anybody around it was good
that she was self-reliant. But Alex was pretty sure
self-reliance could be carried too far. Why not take
the help when it was available and offered? Holly
seemed to push him away for no reason. If positions
were reversed and he normally had a family to support on as little as he knew she was getting by on,
he'd welcome a little help once in a while. Did she
really expect a week or two of pork chops instead
of hot dogs would spoil those kids for life?

What he remembered about Holly told Alex that
she hadn't always been this way. The way Kevin
had talked about Holly, she'd seemed a little more

willing to compromise, to give in, to share the burden with others.

Toiling up the apartment-house stairs, arms laden with groceries, Alex flashed back to his own childhood again. He remembered how routine his mother's life and his own had been during those long periods when his dad was at sea. Not that routine was bad, especially for little kids. They seemed to thrive on it. He knew he had, but life alone with his mother had somehow often slipped from routine to much too quiet.

The celebrations that took place when his father came home along with the rest of his ship's crew always made the old man seem like an even more special individual. And come to think of it, the celebrations also helped to mask, for years, how drab their lives were when he was away. What Jim Wilkins couldn't see didn't exist, and Alex knew his mother made sure that his father saw just what she wanted him to when he was on leave.

The door to Holly's apartment was wide open when he reached her floor. He knew she was probably only seconds ahead of him, but still her carelessness aggravated him. Hadn't they just talked about this? He went through the open door and pointedly kicked it closed behind him without saying a word, making enough noise to remind her to shut it next time.

"I heard that," she called from the kitchen. "Real subtle."

"It wasn't meant to be," he called back.

Her face was flushed when she turned to meet his entrance into the kitchen. "What did you want me to do, shut it in your face so that I'd have to come unlock it again when you knocked? Your expensive ice cream would melt on the countertop while I did that."

"Better melted ice cream than unwanted visitors." Alex put down his pile of bags on the kitchen table. "I shut the trunk, too. It's more work, I know, when we've got another load of groceries to bring up here. But you have to stop announcing to the world what you're doing, Holly."

She looked at him from her place sorting canned goods from the sacks. "I know all that, Alex, really I do. But can't you realize what this does to my life?"

Her violet eyes held traces of harried fear. The expression made Alex want to put an arm around her, find a way to drive away the concern that wrinkled her smooth skin. "I know we weren't really any safer before you came to town. But I could fool myself into thinking we were. That all the ugliness had been left in the big city along with the constant memories of Kevin's death. That maybe, just maybe, I could raise my kids in a normal environment where

I wouldn't have to fear for their safety, and my own, every waking moment.''

It was the sadness in her voice that finally pushed him to action. Alex crossed the small kitchen and put his arms around her, knowing she'd fight the embrace but needing to offer it anyway.

''I'll do anything I can to make it better,'' he told her, meaning every word of it as he wrapped his arms around her thin shoulders. Surprisingly she didn't struggle, but leaned against him. The action caused a thrill of shock to course through him, compounded by the myriad thoughts that crowded his brain at the same time. What made her smell so good—mildly floral with a hint of some kind of spice? Who knew that her dark hair would be so soft, with her head fitting so well under his chin as he pulled her closer?

Merely offering comfort to another human being had never caused feelings like this in him. For once Holly was accepting his help, and it was nearly killing him to give it to her. He wanted to pull back as if he'd touched hot metal instead of the pliant woman who nearly melted in his arms.

''You mean well,'' she murmured. ''And I want to believe you, really I do. It would be so easy if I could believe you. But I know I can't. What I need is some kind of superhero, Alex, and as nice a guy as you are, you're no hero.''

For her he wanted to be one. But Holly's warm body this close to his was causing some very unheroic feelings to assault him. Even as Alex used one finger to tilt her chin up so that their gazes met, he knew he was proving her right. He was no hero if he wanted this badly to comfort them both with a kiss. Still, she didn't fight him, didn't protest at all as he drew ever closer. When their lips met, the actual contact was soft and incredibly sweet. It was all he could do to stay standing upright, not crush Holly between himself and the kitchen cabinets in a much more fervent embrace.

She pulled away first, a rueful smile on her face. "See, what did I tell you? You're no hero, Wilkins. And the fact that I enjoyed that as much as you did proves that I need to hold out for somebody a lot more heroic if I'm going to take any help."

He wanted to tell her that she was wrong. That she couldn't possibly have enjoyed that brief kiss as much as he had. Even if she had, it didn't say anything about either of them except that they were two lonely, needful people who had found each other and connected for a moment. But all he could do was nod dumbly as Holly walked away.

Holly didn't dare look at the bedside clock. It had to be even later now than the last time her sleepless tossing had given her a glance at the bright red numbers. She didn't need to be reminded of how early in the morning it was, and she was still awake.

Not that she could blame all her wakefulness on Alex. She hadn't been sleeping well for the past couple months. It always seemed as if the alarm was ringing just when she'd finally drifted off, some time after two or three in the morning.

But even on her worst nights she hadn't felt this uncomfortable. What had she been thinking yesterday in the kitchen? How could she have let him kiss her? And she had kissed him back, which was another problem. It was one thing to argue that she'd let a handsome man kiss her. Admitting to herself that she'd enjoyed every brief moment of it and was almost sorry when it ended disturbed her even more. How could she have let this happen?

Even worse, why was Alex still under the same roof? He'd promised that last night would be the only time he'd stay at the apartment, but there just wasn't anywhere else in town for him to stay. Annie's bed-and-breakfast at the lighthouse was weeks from being ready for occupants. The motel and hotel opportunities near Safe Harbor were too far from the apartment complex to suit Alex. He still argued that he wanted to be as close as possible to her and the boys in case something happened. Holly was torn between agreeing with him—the fleeting image of

Rico flashing before her—and thinking the whole thing was a massive overreaction.

Of course, the boys had been thrilled to see Alex again when school was over. Holly was almost willing to bet that the man had used their protests as ammunition against her when he'd suggested sleeping in the car tonight. If he didn't want the boys on his side, why had he mentioned sleeping in the car during supper? So he was still on the living-room couch, probably sleeping peacefully, while she tossed and turned in here trying to figure out what to do next.

Maybe Jon-Paul wouldn't mind having a houseguest for a while. His home was nearby, and it was much too large for a single man, anyway. Wasn't he always complaining about how quiet it was when he wasn't working? Of course, that in itself would be a bit of a problem, because Jon-Paul was always working and he probably wouldn't want someone in his house alone for all the hours when he wasn't home himself.

Holly tried to put her wakefulness to good use by brainstorming a good place to put Alex. She ran through all the possibilities for what seemed like a long time, and got nowhere fast. It must have been more effective than counting sheep, though, because the next thing she knew there was sunlight streaming in her window as she bolted upright again.

She crossed the room, then stopped and listened to what was happening. Outside the bedroom door there was definitely a water fight going on. "Now, come on, guys. I'm trying to do your mom a favor here getting you ready for school. Don't mess it up for me, okay?" Alex sounded almost plaintive. Holly, hand on the doorknob, had to stifle a giggle.

So the great, competent Alex wasn't so competent after all. The antics of her dynamic duo got to him, too. She was surprised when the splashing stopped in the hall bathroom and the noise level dropped by quite a bit. "I guess we should, Aidan," she could hear Conor saying. "After all, he made pancakes."

"They weren't as good as Mom's." Aidan defended her, making quick tears well up in her eyes.

"Yeah, but he tried." Conor was always the one with tact. "Besides, Mom will be all grouchy if she wakes up and sees all this water on the floor."

"The last thing I want is for your mom to wake up and be grouchy. So each of you grab a towel." Alex's voice was firm, but not loud. "Anybody big enough to make this much mess is big enough to help clean it up."

That was all she needed to hear to make her let go of the doorknob and head away from the hall, across the bedroom toward her own bathroom. If Alex had the situation that much in control, she was going to let him manage it a little bit longer. Holly had almost forgotten what taking an uninterrupted hot shower felt like, but this sounded like the time to find out.

Of course, her finding out what a long hot shower felt like might make things a little less comfortable for Alex. Holly knew she should be grateful to him for taking care of the boys for this long in the morning. She should probably even offer a prayer of thanks to God for sending this unlikely guardian angel. With a bit of a shock Holly realized that God had been as elusive lately as a good night's sleep. Maybe having Alex here wouldn't be as awful as she'd thought it was going to be. Any man who could put her back in touch with God after a long dry spell had to have his good points.

Chapter Five

"Okay, so tell me all about this," Felicity said when they were rolling silverware in starched napkins before work on Friday. "I want to hear all about this mystery man. All I know is his name. What else is there to know about Alex?" She looked in the direction of the farthest corner of the main dining room, where the object of her attention sat reading the sports page of the local newspaper.

Holly shrugged. "Not much to tell. He worked with my husband, and had some bad news for me regarding a lawsuit surrounding Kevin's death. Now he's camped out on my couch, and I can't get him to leave."

"That hardly sounds like 'not much,'" Felicity said. "I've seen soap operas with thinner plots than that. But it's all I'm going to get out of you, huh?"

Holly felt like agreeing with her young co-worker. It would aggravate Felicity no end, and get Holly off the hook on trying to explain this whole convoluted situation. Still, it wouldn't be very nice to Felicity. And there was the slightest chance that Alex was right about his worries with Rico. If so, having everyone who worked at The Bistro on the lookout might not be such a bad idea.

She'd been hanging around Alex too long, Holly told herself. The fact that she was even considering that he might be right proved that. Still, his caution was catching. She picked up another napkin and bundle of silverware and took a deep breath.

"No, I need to tell you more," she said, watching Felicity out of the corner of her eye. Her admission must have been quite a surprise, because Felicity almost dropped her own silverware bundle. "I'm just trying to decide how far back to start."

"Hey, this is beginning to sound more and more like a soap opera."

"Just wait." Holly knew her expression was grim. "I've said I was a widow, but only Jon-Paul knows anything more than that. My husband was a Chicago police officer. At the time of his death he was working an undercover operation involving drugs and stolen property."

Felicity's eyes were wide. "Wow. Sounds dangerous. Why'd you let him keep doing that?"

Holly shook her head, remembering. "Nobody 'let' Kevin do anything. He was his own man all the way, and he insisted that he could keep his job from impacting his family. Besides, we both wanted me to stay home with the boys as long as possible. With him the only one working, I didn't feel as if I could dictate how he did his job."

For about the hundredth time she wished she had dictated, just that once. Her eyes filled with tears and she stopped rolling silverware. Her fingers were trembling too much to continue. "If I'd said something, maybe he'd still be alive. He was pushing himself, hard, and I can't help thinking that somewhere he slipped. One way or another his cover was blown and a man came to our house. I was just coming home with the boys from a doctor's visit. There was a noise, and someone came running out of the garage."

"You don't have to tell me any more. This is bothering you too much." Felicity had a hand on her shoulder. "In fact, I think you should sit down for a while."

"I'll sit down, but let me keep talking." Now that she was finally telling someone about her past, Holly felt like getting it all out.

"Did you…find him?" Felicity's voice was soft and pained.

"Once I was sure there wasn't anybody else coming out of the garage, I left the boys in their car seats and went to the garage door." She'd heard the sound of gunfire too often to doubt what had happened. The man running away hadn't shown any signs of being shot. "From there I could tell that I didn't want to go any farther. I called the police and the paramedics. They said Kevin had died right after he was shot."

Felicity shuddered. Holly couldn't say anything, because she'd felt that way herself for so long after the event that she knew what was going on in the other woman's mind. "If I'd had a choice, I would have left Chicago then, as soon as I could. But there was a complication. The man who had shot Kevin had made it look like suicide. Only my seeing him run from the garage really proved otherwise. Without my testimony he might have gotten away with murder."

"That's terrible."

"I know. It was the only thing that kept me there and held me together for a while. Once the man was in jail awaiting trial, I moved here. Now Alex tells me that there's been a mistake, and he's been released from police custody. By the time anybody caught the mistake, Rico was long gone."

Felicity was silent, thinking. "Weren't there other guys? Why were you safe as long as this Rico was locked up?"

Holly shrugged. "No honor among thieves, I guess, or in this case drug lords. Salazar was alone when he shot Kevin, and I was the only witness. There was nothing to tie anybody else to the shooting, and with him in jail his friends probably had his share of the profits."

"Do the police think he's on his way here? To do something?" Felicity's eyes were even wider.

"It's possible." Holly closed her eyes. There, she'd actually said it out loud. Unfortunately that possibility sounded more real now that she'd said it. The thought made cold fingers of fear trace her spine. "Alex insists that until he's sure there's no threat to me, he's staying. As in staying in my apartment, which is driving me crazy."

"Hey, if you've got to have a bodyguard, why not a handsome one?" Felicity's smile was lopsided, but definitely present.

"I guess." Holly couldn't tell her that she'd rather have any bodyguard besides Alex, preferably someone old enough to be her father. It would help even more if her bodyguard could be a sort of homely older guy, as well. Maybe like somebody's kindly grandfather. An older man might not be in as good shape as Alex Wilkins, which could slow his response time in a dangerous situation, but given her growing attraction to Alex, she might be willing to make the trade.

* * *

Alex was learning more than he dreamed possible about restaurants and their operation. Just by sitting at his out-of-the-way table at The Bistro and watching the flow of things he picked up a lot. It didn't take long to spot the regulars and notice that Holly was right about one thing—a stranger of Rico's caliber wouldn't get far without being noticed. Still, he was on the lookout for anybody who seemed like a shady customer.

When Jon-Paul took pity on his boredom and put him to work in the kitchen he learned even more. Not that he was trusted with anything complicated. But even trimming up vegetables beat sitting at a table for hours doing nothing. Out front he wasn't any use to anybody, and felt conspicuous to boot. Back here he caught on quickly to the series of mirrors that gave the kitchen workers a fair view into the dining room. Jon-Paul showed him how to spot Holly from almost every angle, and he kept an eye on her whenever he could.

He also got plenty of information about her work habits and the fact that Jon-Paul certainly didn't want to lose her as a server. "She's the best I've got, man. She never misses a shift, and she's the favorite with my older customers. Whatever happens, you've got to let her stay here." The big guy was pretty forceful, especially with a chef's knife in hand.

"That's the general idea," Alex told him. He wondered how much the man knew. Holly didn't appear to have told anybody much of anything, but he figured if anybody knew something about her past, it would be her boss. There was no way to find out by playing dumb. Jon-Paul didn't look like the kind of guy who responded well to anything but the truth, anyway. So Alex needed to fill him in.

"You really think he'll head here?"

"I think someone will. He'd be crazy not to take the chance." The door to the kitchen swung open, and Alex looked in the mirror to try to spot Holly through the open door. She was heading back this way for something, and he was glad to see it. The closer she was, the happier he'd be until this situation resolved itself.

Holly had to fight Alex even to pay the sitter when they got home in the evenings. It was aggravating how much the man tried to take over in her life. Maybe if he'd been gracious about things she would have felt better about it all. But he was so brazen about his insistence on taking care of the groceries, the bills and so much more that it grated on her nerves.

She tried not to squabble in front of Brett, who

went home quickly. If he'd noticed the tension between the adults, it didn't show. He gathered his schoolbooks and went to his own apartment with little more than a quick good-night and instructions on when the next evening would be that he'd watch the boys.

"You can't keep doing that," she said after she shut the door behind the sitter. The chain lock Alex had insisted on adding to the door was fastened, as well. She wanted to give him as little chance as possible to argue where her safety was concerned.

"What, paying the sitter? Why not? I still think you are way too self-reliant when you don't have to be. Let Cook County pick up the expenses while you can. Maybe it will be easier for you that way when I'm not here anymore."

"It can't be too soon."

His face darkened into a scowl. "You keep saying that. Do you think this is any picnic for me, Holly? I have a life, too, that I've abandoned to do this. A nice condo, a comfortable bed, a routine. I'd like to get back to all of that."

Holly felt very small. She hadn't given any thought to what Alex might be missing. She'd been so busy focusing on how her life had changed that she'd forgotten what he might be giving up, too. "Look, I'm sorry. And really embarrassed to be so whiny."

"Forget about it. I've got a lousy temper some-times. You didn't need me snapping at you, either."

"Maybe we're even this time." She held out her hand. "Friends? For now?"

He took it and drew her closer. "Friends. It certainly beats enemies. And maybe later..." Before he finished his sentence, Alex abruptly let go of her hand and froze into stillness.

"What?" Holly hardly got the word out before he held up a hand to silence her. He motioned for her to move across the room, as far from the door as possible. She still didn't hear anything that would have made him this vigilant, but she couldn't argue with his direction, either.

Alex had changed before her eyes. One moment he was calm, easygoing, moving from making up for their little spat into what Holly would have called a mild attempt at flirting with her, perhaps. Then he heard the noise, whatever it was, and any pretense of calm disappeared. His frame was all taut muscle and stillness, alert eyes focused on the door.

Holly's heart jumped in her chest when she saw the doorknob they were both watching turn slowly to the left. Someone was trying the door. She stifled a gasp as the metallic click of a key sliding home echoed in the silence.

Alex was standing in front of the door now, looking through the tiny peephole. He seemed surprised by whatever it was he saw. Motioning for her to stay where she was, and stay quiet, he left the door and went quickly to the coat closet. Holly had never been so glad that her boys were athletic as when Alex pulled the kid-size wooden baseball bat out of the closet.

He went swiftly back to his post at the door and noiselessly removed the chain lock. His left hand had a firm grip on the bat, and his right unlocked the other locks and in one motion pulled the door open with a jerk.

A very young man nearly fell into Holly's living room. "Whoa. Dude, what's going on?" He looked up in puzzlement at Alex, who still had the bat cocked as a weapon. "You are definitely not Matt."

"No, I'm not. Who are you, and why are you trying to break in to this apartment?" He had his hand around the young man's coat collar now, almost lifting him off the ground.

"Hey, I wasn't trying to break in anyplace. I had a key, see? But obviously, not to this apartment. Must have messed up."

"I'd say you did. How about we let the cops sort it out. Holly, you want to call 911 for me?" Alex never took his eyes off the kid he still had firmly in hand.

"That's not really necessary, sir. Like I said, I have a key and everything." The kid's pale-blue eyes were wide now as he realized what kind of trouble he was in. Holly almost felt sorry for him. "I'm looking for Matt Mason. A bunch of us from his old frat house are up here for the weekend. He said we could crash at his place, honest. Even if he wasn't home."

"So that's why you were being so sneaky?"

"Just quiet. It's late, and I didn't want to wake anybody up. And the light out here is really bad...." The young man's voice was getting higher by the moment. Alex hadn't released his grip any.

"Holly? Is there any Matt Mason in the building that you know of?" Alex sounded like the ex-cop he was, not buying a word of the kid's story.

"There actually is. He's across the hall and down one. 2-B, not 2-D," she told them both.

"Why don't we go down there for a minute?" Alex still sounded hopeful that the young man was leading him on. "If your friend is home and can vouch for you, I might let you go with him."

Holly wanted so badly to stand at the open doorway of the apartment to see what happened next. But she knew that Alex would be furious if he came back and found she had breached security that way. So she stood behind the closed door, straining to listen to what was going on across the hall.

There was loud knocking, and some male voices. Alex sounded almost apologetic in tone. In a few minutes he was back, knocking on her door. She even used the peephole herself before letting him in, just to make sure.

"Okay. So he really was Matt Mason's frat brother. But he could have been Rico, or somebody Rico sent. I still don't trust the whole thing. He was just way too quiet with that key, and too ready with the explanation," Alex grumbled as he checked the locks once he was back inside the apartment.

Holly didn't say anything. She could have pointed out that she would have been as quick as possible with an explanation if someone as threatening as Alex were holding her on tiptoe, brandishing a bat. But at the same time she was glad to have him around for a change.

"I'm glad you were here," she told him, reaching up to give him a quick kiss on the cheek. "And I'm glad Aidan's bat didn't have to become a lethal weapon. You would have had a hard time explaining that one to him in the morning."

He looked surprised by both her kiss and her reaction. "Thanks. I'm glad I didn't have to hit the kid myself. Maybe we both ought to get to bed."

"Maybe so," she agreed, heading for the bedroom before she was tempted to show her gratitude for his vigilance in any other way.

In the morning Alex seemed preoccupied. When she laid out her schedule of Saturday-morning errands, laundry and chores, he told her to be as careful as possible without him. "I've got a couple things to do myself," he said, offering no other explanation before he showered and dressed more carefully than usual and disappeared.

He was back by lunchtime. Holly was matching socks and folding clean T-shirts when he knocked on the door. She put down her laundry and let him in. "Well, I touched base with Chief Creasy. He seems to be okay," he said by way of greeting.

"You checked that kid out, didn't you?" Holly knew that's what he had done. She couldn't fault him much, because she suspected that Kevin would have done the same thing in a similar situation.

"Of course. And if he gave me the right name, he is actually who he said he was. If he didn't, he went to a lot of trouble to fake an identity." Alex sounded almost disappointed. "I made one other stop while I was out."

"Oh? I don't see any bags, so you didn't buy me anything for a change."

He smiled brightly, making chills run up Holly's spine. Alex looked too proud of himself to suit her. "Think again. I just had to arrange for delivery."

"Delivery?" The word came out as almost a squeak. "Alex, what did you do this time?"

"I went out and bought a decent sofa. I hope you

like blue floral. It's dark, so it should wear well. I figured that was important, with the boys on the furniture as much as they are.''

"That's really not necessary—'' Holly began, but he cut her off.

"Oh, it definitely is necessary. Because this sofa has a decent innerspring mattress built into the Hide-A-Bed part of it. After last night I figure I'm here for a long time, and that thing over there has got to go.'' He pointed an accusing finger at her tired old sofa.

"I better get to keep it once you're gone,'' she said. "Because I assume you agreed to let the delivery men haul away the old one, and we will need a couch to replace it.''

"Don't worry, they're hauling away the old one. And the new one is yours no matter what. I just couldn't face another night on those creaky springs.''

Holly found herself hiding a smile. "Funny, I thought the lumpy cushions would get to you first. Should I start sorting my laundry someplace else so they can haul this away?''

His answering smile was wide. "You've got time to do this load at least. And we can have lunch. But I did pay the extra for same-day delivery. I couldn't face the thought of one more night on that horror.''

"A man of action.'' Holly wasn't sure what surprised him more—her words, the kiss she blew him afterward, or the clean ball of socks that she sent winging toward his head the moment after she blew the kiss. All she knew was that Alex reacted well to all three. And suddenly her heart felt lighter than it had in months.

Chapter Six

"I never did see him again," Holly said out of the blue two weeks after Alex had bought the new sofa.

"See who?" He wasn't sure what she was talking about. He was too involved in maneuvering out of the grade-school parking lot where before pulling away they'd watched Aidan and Conor get into the building safely. Alex was learning quickly that carpool moms were some of the most aggressive drivers on the planet.

"That kid who knocked at the door. None of his buddies ever turned up at Matt's, either. Maybe there actually was something sneaky going on with him, or you scared him so badly he vanished."

Alex had to smile at the thought of the second

prospect. He didn't think of himself as the kind who would scare kids, even nearly adult ones. In this case scaring the kid would have been okay. Whatever it took to keep him and the rest of the bad elements of society away from Holly's door was okay by him.

"Does this mean you're actually telling me I might have been right about something?" Alex tried not to crow in jubilation.

"I guess it does. Or at least you weren't as wrong as I thought you were." Alex couldn't look over to see if she was teasing him. He had to keep his eyes on the large sport-utility vehicle angling for space in front of him.

"Gee, that's a rousing vote of confidence."

"I could have just kept quiet. I didn't have to say anything about the kid." Now Holly sounded as if she might be a little put out. Great. So much for any gains he might have made in that direction.

"You're right. You didn't have to say anything. I ought to reward that behavior so if anything comes up again, you'll want to mention it to me. Say, if you see any suspicious vehicles in a parking lot, or if you get hang-up calls when I'm not there, anything like that."

"Reward? What did you have in mind?"

Alex headed toward Market Square instead of back to the apartment complex. "I know you won't take much in the way of bribes. So it can't be anything expensive. How about a real breakfast at Harry's Kitchen?''

"Sure. I'd love another cup of coffee, anyway.''

He started looking for a parking space on the square. "Live dangerously and have an omelet or something. A cup of coffee is all you had for breakfast the first time around with the boys and me.''

Holly shrugged. "I don't wake up hungry a lot of mornings. But you know I make up for it later.''

He knew no such thing. Holly's picking at her food was one of the things fueling a growing suspicion in Alex, one he didn't want to face. It was one of the reasons he'd suggested breakfast out to see if someone else's cooking would tempt her more than her own. He parked the car and got out, making sure that they'd both locked their doors behind them.

Harry's Kitchen reminded him of every hometown diner he'd ever been in. Since diners were one of his favorite places, Alex had no arguments with coming in here. The owner waved from behind the counter when they came in, and Alex hoped he wouldn't say anything. Holly didn't need to know where he hung out the few times he left the house without her. And she certainly didn't need to know that he usually met Charles Creasy or another Safe Harbor police officer here to compare notes.

Fortunately there were plenty of other things keeping Harry Connell busy this morning, and Holly didn't seem to notice that Alex had gotten the greeting of a familiar patron. Since the local diner was a no-frills gathering spot, they poured their own coffee, grabbed some cinnamon rolls and Alex congratulated himself on getting Holly to take something besides her coffee. A cinnamon roll wasn't a huge breakfast, but it was more than he'd seen her eat lately. It was a start.

Then they were left to face each other over steaming cups, leaving Alex wondering what to say next. Holly seemed to be looking at him more intensely than usual. The speculative gaze of those unbelievably tinted eyes was unnerving.

For the first few hours after they'd met, Alex was sure that only tinted contact lenses could provide that shade of amethyst. He hadn't remembered Holly's startling eyes from when he knew her before. Of course, then she'd been Kevin's wife, and he probably couldn't have told anybody what color the eyes of any of his friends' or co-workers' wives were.

Now that amethyst gaze was unnerving him. "What? Did I do something stranger than usual?"

That earned him a faint smile. "No. Guess that would be hard to do anyway. You're a pretty strange customer, Wilkins. I was just thinking how little I know about you, really."

"Didn't know you wanted to know more. And

there's really not all that much to tell.'' Not anything he wanted to share, anyway. Alex wished there was something in front of him besides his coffee to keep busy with.

"Oh, come on. Everybody has a life history. I can remember when Kevin and I met, we stayed up one whole night talking about things.'' She looked around at the tiled walls and gleaming chrome of Harry's Kitchen. "Come to think of it, we talked in a place a lot like this one. Do cops and diners just naturally go together?''

"Could be. I like diners because they always look the same. The good ones do, anyway. They're clean, they're simple and I never have to wonder what to order.''

"That sameness, it's important to you, isn't it?'' she asked softly. She was right on target, and it surprised Alex. Not that she could read him so well, exactly, but that he'd let his guard down enough to let her do it.

"I guess it is. My dad was career navy when I was a kid, and I looked for the things that stayed the same.''

"Because nothing much did.''

"Right. How do you know that?''

Holly shrugged. "Same kind of childhood. With me it was just the corporate transfer thing. I think I went to six different schools between kindergarten and eighth grade.''

"Ouch. Been there. What happened in eighth grade that changed things?''

Holly's clear gaze clouded over a little. "My dad had a heart attack. After he was gone, Mom insisted we were staying in one place so that my sister and I could finish school. But it was just a place, you know? Not home or anything.''

So they'd both lost parents as teenagers. And they apparently shared a lot of feelings, at least about having a nomadic childhood. It was on the tip of Alex's tongue to tell her that, but something held him back. This was the most Holly had said about herself, and he was more anxious to hear about her life than he was to share the details of his own.

"How did you meet Kevin? It must have been really appealing to you that he'd never been more than fifty miles from home in his whole life.''

"Now, that isn't true. He'd been as far as New York City on vacation. And Disney World. I remember him mentioning both.'' Holly smiled at the memory. "But yeah, it was an attraction. He was so grounded. There I was checking out another place out of the dozens of places I'd been and for him community college thirty miles from home was this giant adventure.''

She looked down and swirled her coffee around

in her cup. "How did you know that much about him, anyway?"

"He talked a lot about some things. Back in the days when we were both on the same teams for things like stakeouts, I heard a lot about his life."

"More than he heard about yours, I'll bet." Those eyes were boring holes in him again.

"Yeah, probably. I liked listening to his stories. They were so normal. I mean, he had a regular childhood, complete with a kid sister and a puppy."

"You were envious, too, weren't you?" Holly said it softly.

"I guess I was. The closest I ever came to memories like his was watching family sitcoms on cable TV. I mean, before I knew Kevin Douglas I didn't think anybody really grew up like that, you know?"

Her eyes were damp now, and Alex cursed himself silently for bringing on this emotion. "Oh, I know. Believe me, I know. I've been reminded more than once how I messed up that perfect life."

That brought him out of his own emotions. "You? What are you talking about?"

She took a slow, deep breath and closed her eyes for a moment. "They blamed me for it. His family. His mother and sister, especially. His sister told me at Kevin's funeral that if I'd kept working after the twins were born Kevin would still be alive."

"That's the craziest thing I ever heard." Alex had to struggle to keep his voice down.

"No, not really. I can see her point." Holly was incredibly calm. Alex couldn't believe she would have listened to something that vicious. "He was stretching himself to the limit. Working a part-time job in security between his shifts for Narcotics left him mentally drained all the time. If I had taken some of that load off, maybe he wouldn't have died."

"Holly, that's ridiculous." Alex had to take hold of her hands across the table to get her to look him in the eye. "Nothing you did caused Kevin's death. Nothing any of us could have foreseen without knowing a lot more than we did about Rico could have prevented that from going down."

"I don't know. Kevin was so smart. And he loved his job so much. I just can't see how he'd make a mistake that big, letting Rico find him like that, find out where he lived...."

"I can't, either. But I don't think it was a mistake made from exhaustion. I think maybe Kevin over-estimated his own ability to handle the situation, or underestimated Rico. And neither one of those things can be blamed on you."

"If you say so." Holly drew her hands away. She didn't look as if she believed him.

They finished up their meal mostly in silence. He

couldn't bring himself to nag Holly even when three-quarters of her roll remained on her plate when they got up from the table.

Alex didn't know what else to say. He could hardly imagine what it was like to walk around in her position each day. Not only did she have the crushing weight of raising two kids alone, but she carried that burden of guilt about her husband's death, as well. It would have to be overwhelming.

After their disastrous breakfast, Holly didn't know what to say to Alex. She felt as if she'd made a fool of herself, spilling all her problems and crying in public. He could barely look at her afterward. Obviously he wanted nothing to do with her. She was relieved when he said he had business to take care of and took her back to the apartment. It was good to lose herself in cleaning and the other normal tasks of a regular day when she didn't have to work the lunch shift.

Alex was weaving himself into the fabric of their lives much too quickly and much too deeply to suit her. Just looking around the apartment, she could see his presence everywhere. Not only was there the new sofa, but his things had a way of creeping into every room. Wiping the kitchen countertops, Holly could count a set of mugs, the high-grade coffee and the jar full of pens and pencils that hadn't been there before Alex came. And that was only one room.

The desk in the living room where the kids drew pictures or she usually paid bills now held Alex's laptop computer most of the time. She'd even caught him more than once teaching the boys to play games on it when he'd finished up whatever business he was dealing with. The suitcase stowed under the coffee table wasn't a nuisance, exactly, but it was another reminder of the man living in her apartment. So were the things that were in the medicine cabinet in the boys' bathroom, and the extra towel on the hook there. Alex even did his own laundry, so she couldn't very well accuse him of being a burden. But there were reminders everywhere that she was no longer alone.

She couldn't deny that Alex was here, and probably here to stay for a while. But she didn't have to like the idea, and she didn't have to be so friendly to him. From now on, Holly decided, she'd try to treat him like what he really was—a man doing a job that had to be done. It probably wasn't any more pleasant for him than it was for her to have their lives mingled like this. Her outburst today was a good place to start in redrawing the lines between them.

It was bad enough that Alex wouldn't treat this assignment like the job it was and take a day off once in a while. But no, he wasn't going to trust anybody else to keep an eye on her, of that Holly was already certain. She felt fortunate that she'd convinced him that she could function like a normal adult long enough to be alone in her own apartment once in a while.

Luxuriating in doing just that, she almost missed picking up the boys at school on time. She didn't know what would make Alex more aggravated—the fact that she would pick them up alone since he hadn't gotten home yet, or waiting for him, thereby calling attention to herself. It would bother her more to be late, so she chanced Alex's wrath by dashing to school on her own.

She made it to school just before the kids started pouring out of the building. They came out into the crisp air bouncing down the sidewalk, cheeks pink. Holly wanted to scoop them both up and hug and kiss them instead of just motioning them into the back seat, where they got into their safety boosters. But she knew what kind of response something like that would get. Even kindergarten boys did not welcome public displays of affection from their mothers, so she refrained whenever possible.

"So, how was your day, guys?"

"Great!" Conor said. "Where's Alex?"

His question made her flinch. The man had been part of their life for only a short time, and already the boys were counting on him. This could not be a good thing. It only strengthened her resolve to try to keep Alex at arm's length for a while. "He had to do some errands. He'll be back before suppertime."

"Okay. Are you going to stay home tonight?" Aidan sounded suspicious.

"Nope. I have to work." Holly tried to keep her tone as casual as possible. No sense in them knowing that it nearly destroyed her to miss so much of their childhood.

"Can Alex stay home with us, then?" Conor just wasn't going to let this go.

"I don't think so. Brett will be there like always."

"That's okay, I guess. I just wanted to tell Alex about the movie. We saw a really neat movie today."

"Oh?" Holly wondered why he couldn't just tell her about the "really neat movie." She'd always been good enough before.

"Yeah." It must have been a good movie for Aidan to chime in, too. "It had lions. Wanna hear me roar?" Before she could answer he was roaring, and there was no more discussion on the way home. Just two wild things in the back seat, roaring, while their mother tried to get home in one piece.

Alex didn't show up until Holly was almost ready to go to work. She didn't know whether to be relieved to see him or angry that he'd come back just in time to escort her. She was beginning to feel as if she was the criminal instead of Rico. It was definitely *her* life that was being disrupted by all this.

The boys all but flung themselves at Alex the minute he came through the door. Holly wanted to shout at all of them—Alex for coming here and turning their lives upside down, and her boys for getting so attached to him so quickly. None of it felt right.

Instead she pushed her anger away and said as little as possible. She got dressed for work while Alex entertained the boys. He seemed a little put out that she wasn't paying him much attention, but he'd just have to get over it, she thought. Brett came, and she and Alex left.

She let him drive them both to The Bistro, where he was allowed to park in the back now like a regular employee. "You're awful quiet tonight. I expected at least to be grilled about where I'd been all day," he said, sounding hopeful.

"No need. I figure that if you had something important to tell me, you'd tell me. Rico's still on the loose?"

"Yes."

"And you've got no clue where he is, right?"

"There's a couple leads. Nothing firm enough to send anybody in for an arrest."

"Then nothing much has changed, has it?" Holly

asked. Nothing much had, as far as Rico was concerned, but for her quite a bit had changed. She had decided that there was no way to let Alex into her life. He'd already worked his way in much too successfully without her permission, and it was time to turn the situation around.

"I guess nothing has changed," Alex said slowly. "It sure sounds like something has changed from your perspective. And I have no clue what has happened to make you even more removed than you were before. However, I don't expect you're going to tell me, either."

Holly felt like telling him he had that right. But that would only lead to more discussion on a subject where she'd already made up her mind. She used to be a strong person before Alex Wilkins had shown up at her door, hadn't she? It was time to find that strength again, and put it to her own use. So she stayed quiet for the rest of the short trip to The Bistro.

Seeing Alex get almost as warm a greeting there as she did only strengthened her resolve to start getting him out of her life. They were somehow becoming a team in people's minds. And that wasn't good. She was alone now, and likely to be alone for quite some time to come, managing her life and raising her boys. There was just no room for Alex in her life. If she let him in now, she risked having to fill the gaping hole he'd leave when he left.

Holly knew he'd leave, and when she least expected him to. Rico would be found, probably somewhere hundreds of miles from here, totally unconcerned with her. And then Alex would be gone and she'd be back to square one. No, worse than that. If she got any more used to him being here, any more attached to his presence, she'd be brokenhearted again when he left, just as she'd been when Kevin died and left her alone. Because Holly knew herself well enough to know that she was getting very used to Alex and his quirky ways. She was depending on him far, far too much. If she could let him into her life this quickly, it was only a matter of time before she let him into her heart, as well. And that just could not happen.

Chapter Seven

Holly dragged through the next week or so, keeping her resolve to shut Alex out as much as possible. It wasn't easy. He'd already become too much of a part of their lives for that to work very well. The boys loved having him around. It was clear that the male support she'd tried to provide by having Brett as a baby-sitter and involving different men from church in their lives just wasn't enough. They needed a man around all the time, and welcomed Alex with open arms.

When she was being objective she could see why they took to him so readily. Alex was fun to be with, especially for little boys. He'd get down on the floor and wrestle, like Brett would, but he could also provide authority in a way that Brett was too young to manage. He was also better in the boys' eyes than the other adult males they came in contact with. After all, he didn't come at them with booster-shot needles like Robert Maguire, and he was much more accessible than Reverend Burns. And, at least to hear Conor tell it, Alex could scramble eggs better than she could, so he won even more points with one of her sons.

She could see all three of them giving her questioning looks when she begged off on joining their board games or judging their goofy-face-making contests. Even though she couldn't find a way to explain her new standoffish behavior to her sons, she felt as if she had to continue with it. It just wouldn't do for all three of them to depend this much on anyone again.

She probably couldn't stop the boys from depending on someone as attractive to them as Alex. That meant that when Alex finished this assignment and went back to Chicago she'd have a lot of anger and hurt feelings to deal with from her guys. But it would be much easier than dealing with her own broken heart at the same time. As long as she held firm on not getting any more involved with Alex, she'd be all right.

She kept telling herself that through long days of work and even longer nights alone, listening to him watch sporting events on the television on the other side of the wall that separated the two of them.

Knowing Alex was on the other side made that wall seem very thin to her. Holly even seriously considered moving her bed so that it didn't back up to the inside wall of the apartment just so she wouldn't be so aware of Alex in the next room. But where she was let her hear the boys if they woke during the night, and kept her away from the colder outside walls of the apartment when the wind coming off the lake whipped around the building. Besides, she couldn't move the bed without help, and she had no desire to explain her yen to move furniture to Alex.

He was looking for explanations anyway, even without any furniture-moving. Every time Holly pulled away, either physically or verbally, Alex gave her a questioning look. So far he hadn't cornered her for a long talk, but she knew it was just a matter of time.

Until it happened she could keep herself busy, and she did. There was always plenty of laundry to do while she was home, and straightening-up around the apartment. With Alex providing the amount of groceries he insisted on, it meant there was plenty of cooking to do, as well. She didn't think he was buying cake mixes and the ingredients for chocolate chip cookies just because he wanted them. He seemed to get as much pleasure as she did over watching the boys scout out the kitchen when they came home from school. Having a mom who baked cookies was a treat the boys didn't remember. The last time she'd really had time to do that had been when they were much smaller, when Kevin was still alive and working.

Even the little pleasures like that one that Alex was able to provide just got under Holly's skin. Surely she should be able to handle details like that without Alex or any other man to help, shouldn't she? When she was honest with herself she had to admit that it was probably impossible for her to provide, alone, all the comforts a two-parent family could afford for her boys. It still needled her to have Alex provide things so readily. How did a single guy who had never had a wife or kids know so instinctively how to fit in? If he'd been more of an annoyance it would have been much easier to dislike him.

Even going to work didn't provide Holly with a total escape. Alex followed her there, of course, and he was fitting in there as well as he did at home. He and Jon-Paul were quickly forming a friendship, and he'd even won over the normally prickly Felicity. Alex won additional points by offering to pick up all three grade schoolers one Friday and bring them back to the restaurant while their mothers finished serving a large, late lunch crowd.

When Alex's car drove up with his precious

cargo, Holly was in the kitchen where she could see the back parking lot. She was happy to see that all three kids got out of the back seat, and only after Alex came around and opened a door, proving that he used the childproof locks. The threesome bounded out of the car, and all four headed up the outside stairs to the kitchen entrance. "We're back. Did you miss us?" Alex called out.

The kids looked up at him as if he was a bit strange. "We didn't come back. We weren't here before," Jasmine told him, lecturing like the mature young woman she considered herself at six. She even shook her head much as Holly had seen her mother do it.

Alex didn't look as if he felt reprimanded. In fact, he didn't look much older than the threesome he was escorting. If Holly hadn't been trying to ignore him, it would have been enchanting. "Oh, that's right. The rest of you were at school. I'm the only one who's been here today. Anybody else hungry?"

"Oh, no, that's not part of the bargain," Holly said. "Jon-Paul doesn't have to feed this crew. They know enough to sit over there and do homework for ten minutes or so, and then we'll all go home."

"Too late," Jon-Paul called from the other side of the kitchen. "I got the ice cream out when I saw them pull into the parking lot. And homemade chocolate sauce, guys. I had plenty left over from the

Rotary lunch you two just finished working. Surely everybody can have a quick sundae before you leave, can't they?''

Holly looked at Felicity. ''I think we've been had. We're the bad people for sure if we argue with this, aren't we?''

Felicity grinned. ''Yeah. And I can't see turning down a hot fudge sundae right now, can you?''

Holly could, but she knew the kids, and probably Alex, would never turn down dessert. So she shrugged and gave Alex as sharp a look as she could get away with. Of course it had no effect whatsoever. ''Go supervise some hand washing, will you? Some nice, quiet hand washing and a nice, quiet trip back to the kitchen. The Rotary president and his board are still wrapping up their meeting in that private room.''

''Yes, ma'am,'' Alex said. The wink he gave her on the way out of the room nearly undid her.

Once they got back and started eating ice cream, Holly tried to hurry things along so that they could all get home. It was difficult to hurry kids eating ice cream. Everybody had to regale the table with how their day had gone. Conor was trying to tell them all something more about the lion movie or video or whatever, which Holly never did follow. Maybe it was the longer shift or maybe it was just the wrong time of day, but she almost sagged in relief when it was finally time to go home.

The drive seemed to take twice the time it usually did, even though the weather was clear. And getting the boys inside the apartment and settled took forever.

"You look beat," Alex said once she was sitting on the couch looking through Conor's and Aidan's homework folders. "Why don't I pop for pizza tonight and give you a break?"

"I don't need a break. I've been getting nothing but breaks, and I need some good honest work to get back in shape," Holly said.

Alex sat down at the other end of the couch. She really hoped he didn't come any closer. He was difficult to resist at a distance, and almost impossible to resist from close up. Today in tan cords and a flannel shirt he looked particularly cuddly. It wasn't a term she would have thought of using for a sharp-edged cop turned lawyer a month ago, but with Alex it fit. Especially when he got that concerned look in his eyes, as he had right now.

"I have to disagree with you," he said, sounding far more serious than she'd expected. Holly's heart sank as she realized that they were finally going to have to have the talk she'd been putting off for days. "You haven't gotten nearly enough breaks lately. In fact, you won't let me do anything anymore. What's up?''

She tried to look involved with the homework folders, but there wasn't anything that absorbing about coloring pages and worksheets about the letter *Q*. ''Nothing's up. At least, that's the way I'd like it.''

''Maybe so, but I'm real uncomfortable. I thought we were really fitting in together until a few days ago. Then suddenly we're back to square one again. No, worse, because I wasn't getting this much cold shoulder from you when I first got here. I know I'm a clueless male, but I can't figure out what I did this time, Holly.''

He looked so concerned and vulnerable it nearly brought tears to her eyes. *You cared,* she felt like saying. In the instant she thought it, Holly knew that was the problem. Alex cared, and it had been such a very long time since anyone truly had cared that she'd built up a huge defense against it.

The tears came now whether she fought them or not. For a change Alex didn't spring right up and move in closer. A woman's tears appeared to unnerve him. He sat on his end of the couch looking more and more uncomfortable. Holly could feel him stiffening even in the distance between them. ''I'm sorry. I didn't mean to do that,'' she said, but she couldn't stop the tears, either. What was wrong with her? She felt like crying a lot, but she never gave in to it like this.

"I know you didn't. And it's all right. Really." After a few more minutes Alex got up off the couch and walked into the kitchen. Holly fumbled around for a tissue and tried to compose herself. By the time he came back she'd managed to pull herself together a little.

"All right, I've got things to say now." Alex looked the way she expected him to, composed and determined. "You can argue some other time. I called Brett and he's okay with coming tonight. He and the guys will get pizza, and you and I are going out. Someplace outside Safe Harbor, where nobody knows you or me, so if you cry at the table again, it won't matter. Because we are going to talk."

He'd given her several ultimatums before, but Alex had never looked more serious. Holly knew from experience that she didn't have any room for argument. "How much time do I have to get ready?"

"One hour. And this is progress. You didn't even argue."

"Would it do any good?"

For the first time, he smiled. "No, not really. But you will have to tell me where to go, because I still don't know the area outside this little town."

Oh, she'd tell him where to go, all right, Holly

thought as she went to her bedroom to get ready. Too bad that it wouldn't have any effect, no matter what she told him.

How long would it take him to break the ice here? Alex looked around the restaurant. It was just the right kind of place to be if they had a serious discussion. The family-style pizza place was cheery and loud, and neither of them would probably care if they never came here again. Nobody would notice their talking in the booth, because there were too many things going on around them.

"Good choice," he told Holly. "Not romantic, but then I didn't plan on it being a romantic kind of place. I don't think it's going to be that kind of night."

Holly's smile was wan. "At least I don't have to worry about you proposing, then."

Ouch. Even as a joke that was hard to take. Alex knew his answering smile was just as weak as hers. "True. At least not proposing marriage, which is what you meant. I do have a proposal for you."

"Cute, Wilkins. But you didn't drag me twenty miles from home for jokes and puns."

It looked as if they were going to get to the serious stuff before the pizza came, Alex thought. He hoped Holly still had an appetite once they finished talking.

Okay, here it went. "You're right. I didn't. We've been in pretty close quarters for a while now. I feel like I've gotten to know you fairly well on some levels."

"Not on all levels, or we wouldn't have come all the way over here for a talk we could have had on my couch. Or your couch in my living room."

"It's your couch." Alex could see her already trying to change the subject even before she was sure what the subject was. He could tell from her darting eyes that she was nervous. He felt like reaching over and taking her hand. The urge got strong enough that he followed up on it. What he was going to say was tough enough. Might as well try to calm them both down.

"But I didn't come here to talk about furniture. I came to talk about you." He kept holding her hand. It was a little cool and seemed to be trembling slightly. "Like I was saying, I've seen a lot of you. Can I point out a few things I've noticed?"

"As long as they're not too embarrassing. I don't snore, do I?"

She seemed genuinely concerned. "Not so that I can hear it in the next room. But then, one of the things I'd like to point out is that I don't think I'd know if you snored, because I don't think you sleep all that much."

"So what? How many single moms with a demanding job do you think sleep well at night?"

"Everybody sleeps well sometimes. Almost everybody."

She looked across the table at him, defensive and guilty. Holly opened her mouth as if there was something she wanted to say, but the young waiter arrived bringing their pizza.

For a few moments all their conversation stopped while they reached for napkins, got slices of pizza and settled back down again. Alex took a bite while it was still hot, savoring the meal. He knew what he'd see when he looked over at Holly's plate. As he expected, it was untouched.

"How's your pizza?" he asked when he got a chance.

Holly didn't quite glare at him, but it was close. "Fine. I guess. I'm a little nervous to eat."

"There's always an excuse, Holly. You're too busy. You ate at work. The boys need your attention." He reached over and took her hand again. "The truth is that just like you don't sleep a whole lot, you don't eat much most of the time either, do you?"

"Where is this going, Alex? Is there a point to all this?"

"There is. And it's a pretty serious one. I know you've got a lot to be concerned about. Your life isn't easy. It wasn't easy before I came and added more burdens to it. But I think you've got more problems than just being a single mom when you didn't choose to be, or even having a bad guy like Rico after you.''

"Like what?" She leaned in toward him, as if she were eager to know. Alex had to face the surprising thought that perhaps Holly had no idea where he was headed with all of this.

He took a deep breath and tried to find the right way to phrase this now that he was here. He needed help with the right words. Alex realized he should have given this even more consideration, maybe even some really deep prayer, before he tackled it. It was too late now for anything but a quick request for guidance from God before he plunged in.

"This is tough for me, Holly. What I see is a picture of someone suffering from something serious. I think you are deep into a depression. Not just feeling a little down, but a real medical problem. And I think you should get some help.''

Okay, so he'd finally said it. Once the words were out Alex felt a tremendous sense of relief, as if something he'd been carrying around that was too heavy was suddenly lifted from him. Judging from her expression, he figured he'd just transferred the burden to Holly.

She was pale and looked stunned. "So you think

I'm crazy? Is that it? Thanks, Wilkins. Thanks for nothing.'' She tore from his grasp and pulled away from the table. Alex got up to follow her, but instead of heading for the exit she went through the one door he wasn't about to follow her through in the entire restaurant.

He leaned against the wall of the hallway where phones and a drinking fountain stood between the rest-room doors. He wasn't going anywhere until Holly came out where they could resume this discussion.

There was no repairing her makeup. Holly looked into the mirror again, giving up on doing anything but scrubbing her blotchy face with a paper towel. So far several other women had come and gone in the room, but none had done more than give her a glance. Each time they'd left, looking uncomfortable.

She was going to have to go out there eventually. Alex would wait for as long as it took. She knew that about him. What she didn't know was where he'd come up with such an outrageous idea. The man had barely known her a few weeks. How could he possibly think she was mentally ill?

Okay, so she didn't sleep all the best. And she might cry more than she had before. Perhaps her clothes were a little loose on her. Did that all really add up to anything? Alex was seeing things that weren't there. He was so involved in being an investigator, in solving problems, that he'd gone and created one where there wasn't a problem to solve. She would just have to push open that door and tell him that.

Holly looked at her reflection in the mirror. The young woman she saw there looked like a haunted old soul. "I am not depressed," she whispered. "I am *not* at all depressed." The deep violet eyes stared back at her, with bruised-looking shadows underneath them echoing their color. Great. Not only was she not ready to convince Alex that his idea was all wrong, but she couldn't even convince her own reflection. At this rate it was going to be a very long ride back to Safe Harbor tonight.

Chapter Eight

It was snowing on the way back to Safe Harbor, just a light snow of the kind that Alex had begun to think of as normal. The roads weren't covered yet, and he didn't even have to put the windshield wipers on high. It was kind of mesmerizing, watching the wiper blades and driving into the snowy darkness. Holly was quiet, as she had been since they'd left the restaurant.

"Sooner or later, you're going to have to say something," he told her softly. There wasn't any answer from her right away. Alex was surprised that his suggestion had caused this strong a reaction. He'd expected some argument, because with Holly there was always an argument. But he hadn't expected that she'd bolt for the ladies' room and hide out for so long, then come out totally silent. It would have been better to have the argument.

"Maybe I have to say something and maybe I don't." Holly's answer was as soft as his statement had been. "What if I believe that you're totally wrong?"

"Then at least say that. But if I'm so totally wrong, why did you go hide out where I couldn't talk to you for over twenty minutes before you came out?"

Holly made an inarticulate sound of frustration. "Is this what arguing with lawyers is always like? Or are you just a stubborn, obnoxious individual aside from being a lawyer?"

"Both, maybe. Nobody ever told me I was easy to get along with, even before law school," Alex admitted. Of course, there hadn't been that many people close to him in the past decade or so who would have known how easy, or hard, he was to get along with. He just hadn't let that many people in.

"I'd have to go along with that. You're no prize to get along with, Wilkins." Holly settled back into her silence, which lasted until they pulled up in the parking lot of the apartment complex.

Once Holly got out of the car Alex decided to press his luck. He went around to her side and put his hands on her shoulders. "Make no mistake about it, we will talk more about this, Holly. And please, if you can only trust me about one thing, trust me when I tell you I'm only doing this because I care about you." She looked so vulnerable in the darkened lot, snow falling into her sooty eyelashes, that Alex wished he could hold her and kiss her.

He settled for a quick kiss on the cheek, drawing back before she could protest. "I know, Alex," was all she said before they headed inside.

Since the evening hadn't turned out to be a long one, the boys were still up. They both bounded off the couch when they heard Holly and Alex come through the door. Conor, as usual, was doing most of the talking.

"Hey, Mom, guess what? Brett knows about the lion movie. And guess what? It's a book, too. And he has it. And we went downstairs with him and got it, and he's reading it to us!" Conor was bouncing with excitement.

"That's great," Holly said. It sounded to Alex as if she were forcing the enthusiasm a bit. He could see only the back of her neck between her hair and the dark coat, and he wondered if her face was flushed or if, as she sounded, she was teary-eyed.

Still ahead of him, she went over to the couch where Brett was closing up his book. "Okay, so what kind of nature story is this lion movie, or book, or whatever?" She seemed confused when Brett laughed.

"No nature book, Mrs. Douglas. Just a lot of great stories."

"And they're about lions?" That prompted another laugh from Brett.

"Not all about lions. But it's the lion book, Mom. And it's just like our house." Conor was still impersonating a jack-in-the-box.

"The lion book is just like our house?" Holly sounded as puzzled as Alex knew he would be.

"Yeah. Show her, Brett," Conor said.

"I don't know about how it's like your house, Conor. But it's a really good book. *The Lion, the Witch and the Wardrobe,*" Brett said. How that was like Holly's apartment Alex wasn't sure. Maybe you had to be five to understand that bit of logic.

It seemed to have Holly struggling for an answer, as well. "Oh. So that's the lion movie. And the lion book. I should have thought about it that way. But Conor, I still don't see how that's like our house at all."

"The winter part, Mom." As if that explained everything.

Finally Aidan, who had been relatively quiet, bouncing around with his brother, stopped and looked at her. "Right. Always winter and never Christmas. That's like our house."

The sting of the child's statement, made in such a matter-of-fact way, made Alex wince. He wondered what it could possibly be doing for Holly. She sat down on the couch; he wasn't sure if it was from shock or just tiredness. If he had to guess, he would have said it was a little bit of both.

"Oh. I see." Her beautiful violet eyes held a bruised look. "Always winter and never Christmas. Maybe Uncle Alex and I have more to talk about than I thought."

Her statement gave Alex hope. But they ended up not saying much at all even after he'd paid Brett and the sitter had left, and both boys were tucked into bed.

Alex thought that for once it might be best to leave Holly with her thoughts. Maybe after that bald statement coming from her own kids she would see what he had meant in the restaurant. He hoped so, anyway.

Always winter and never Christmas. And that, to her children, was just like home. Holly lay awake hours after tucking Aidan and Conor in, thinking about that statement. Before they had gotten home, she'd been ready to dismiss Alex's idea that she might be depressed. At least, she wasn't ready to admit that she was depressed enough to need some sort of medical help.

Anybody could see that her life was depressing, and had been for a while. Raising two kids alone was exhausting work. Even with the support she got from her church and the Safe Harbor Women's League, she *did* feel alone most of the time. Maybe she was to blame for some of that loneliness, because she didn't go out seeking help or companionship. Alex would say so, anyway.

Surely the things that Alex had ticked off in the restaurant didn't really mean a serious medical problem. She was just a little tired, and stressed. Maybe she was working too hard, and not paying attention to her own health nearly as much as she was everybody else's. It still didn't seem to her that those things should automatically add up to a serious medical problem.

Still tossing, Holly looked at the clock. It was after one and she was still wide-awake. If she listened intently she could hear a little bit of noise in the living room. Alex was still awake just a few yards away.

Well, since he was still awake, too, she decided to go talk this out. It certainly wasn't helping just lying there awake. Holly got out of bed and groped in the dark for the robe at the end of the bed. The oversize T-shirt and flannel pants she was sleeping in were hardly risqué, but she didn't want to give Alex any ideas. Besides, it was cold in the middle of the night.

She wrapped the robe around her, thinking that it

was even more disreputable than her pajamas. Kevin had given it to her the first Christmas of their marriage, and the fleecy fabric was almost worn through in spots. It had been stretched out of shape by her pregnancy with the twins, and had seen a lot of abuse when she was up nights with them as babies. It still felt comforting to wrap the ratty old thing around her.

Alex was stretched out in the made-up sofa bed, the flickering television the only light in the room. "Am I keeping you up? I'm sorry. I thought I was being quiet."

"No, it's not you. It's me." Holly thought that maybe Alex had plenty to do with keeping her up tonight, but he wasn't the total cause. And it certainly wasn't his quiet television-watching that was keeping her up. "I couldn't sleep thinking about what you said earlier, and then what Aidan said."

She sat in the chair closest to the couch and tucked her legs up under her to stay warm. The action wrapped her robe around her, and she felt as if she was wrapped in a giant security blanket. Given the way she felt tonight, that was all right. There probably wasn't a security blanket anywhere big enough to hold all of her insecurities right now.

"How do you feel about that?"

"Which part of it? What the guys said, or what you said? I still think you're off base."

"I meant what Aidan said. Little kids pretty much say what they feel. And even if you don't believe what I said, it had to be pretty brutal to hear almost the same thing coming from him."

He didn't mince words. Holly wouldn't expect him to. She might as well be as honest with him as he was with her. "Yes, it hurt. Especially when I realized that both boys felt the same way about the lion book, as they called it."

She snuggled up under her robe, looking for more comfort than she could get from it. "I still think you're wrong. But what my boys said made me think about it some more. And I'm willing to truly consider what you said."

"Thank you. That's what I wanted to begin with." He reached out, and Holly could feel the warmth of his hand through the fabric of her robe.

"Why? Why did you want that? We haven't known each other all that long. Why care that much?" It was one of the questions that had kept her awake tonight. It might have been the biggest one. She could accept that maybe Alex saw something in her that made him think she was depressed. But what she couldn't see was why he bothered to do all this.

"Why should I care that much? A couple different reasons, Holly. One is that I've lived here now for close to a month. I've gotten to know you, and your children. I care for you, and I want to see what's best for you."

"And you think this is the best? To tell me that I have a serious medical problem and need help?"

"Yes, I do. Depression doesn't just affect one person. It touches a whole family when it touches one person, and until you get better, your sons are going to feel the impact of your problem."

Somehow Holly could feel intensity in Alex that she hadn't expected. "There's more to it than that, isn't there? I believe you care for us, Alex. I'm not questioning that. But I just have to feel that there's something else going on here that made you say something."

His hazel eyes widened. "Yeah. There is, I guess. But how can you tell? I'm not exactly somebody who keeps his feelings on the outside."

"No, you're not. But then, remember my background."

"Seen one cop, you've seen them all?" He withdrew his hand and looked hurt.

"No, that's not what I meant at all. Do you really think I'm that shallow?"

He didn't meet her gaze right away. "No, not really. But I was a little taken aback when you asked me if there was something else going on with me. Maybe our discussions tonight have gotten to me more than I thought."

Holly knew her answering smile was wry. "You mean I didn't have the market cornered on emotional outbursts tonight? I am really sorry I went and hid in the ladies' room. At least, I'm sorry I stayed in there so long. Maybe I needed a little time to compose myself, but I bet you were ready to send in a search party."

His grin was quick. "If our server hadn't been a guy, you would have had company. I tried to ask one woman if you were in there, but it's funny, most women resent being accosted by a strange man outside that particular doorway."

Holly laughed, trying to keep her voice soft so she didn't wake up the boys. "I'll bet. But Alex, you're changing the subject here. You're being very entertaining, but you're not answering my question. What happened in your past that made tonight even more important to you?"

His expression went back to serious, and Alex settled against the back of the couch. He looked up toward the ceiling. Holly wondered if he was trying to compose himself or just reflecting on the best way to tell his story. She could see that something important was about to happen between them. The air in the room felt charged with emotion and Alex's muscles were taut.

"I haven't said much about my family. I told you my dad was career navy."

Holly nodded, trying to give him just enough encouragement to keep going. "That's why you moved around so much."

"Yeah. Most of the time it was just Mom and me. It was pretty quiet. I see a lot of the way we got along when I look at your apartment."

Holly winced. "Ouch. Does that mean including the boys and their wintry description of our home life?"

"It does." There was a muscle in Alex's cheek that was doing a slow dance. Holly couldn't resist reaching out to smooth the skin, make contact with him. He leaned into her touch and sighed. "We weren't poor or anything. And I don't mean to say that things were horrible or anything."

"Just not what they could have been, maybe." That part Holly could clearly see in her existence, and in her children's. It was the one thing that made her take Alex's statements more seriously.

"That's the right way to put it. And I think all the moving around let my mom hide what was going on from my dad for years longer than if he'd come home every night like the typical suburban dad."

"Do you think she was depressed? Is that it?" Holly found herself leaning forward, wanting to know. Her hand was on his shoulder now and she could feel him flex and tense as he thought about it all.

"I know she was. Remember, twenty years ago nobody talked about mental illness quite the way they do today. It was a pretty hushed, embarrassing subject. And she didn't have much in the way of close friends or family to keep track of her."

His gaze was past the far wall now, and his voice soft, tight. Holly was getting the most awful downcast feeling. "She didn't make it, did she, Alex?"

He looked down, shaking his head. "Things got worse when I was in high school. I tried to talk to her, tell her I was worried. But I was a fourteen-year-old kid. What could I say, what did I know? My dad was away on another tour, of course. Oddly enough, she waited to actually do anything until he came home. We had Christmas, and my fifteenth birthday, and four days later my mother killed herself."

The finality of his words made Holly shiver. "That's terrible. Did you know, then, that it was suicide? Are you sure now?"

"We knew. She left a note, and my dad read it to me, more than once. He just couldn't believe it had all happened." Alex was still staring through the opposite wall somewhere, seeing that pain-filled scene of his adolescence. Holly didn't know whether to hug him or not right now. He looked like a man who wanted to hold on to a little of his pain, to keep the memory there for a while.

So she sat back, trying to warm herself while she listened. She let Alex tell her all he wanted of his story, the painful mess of his sophomore year with a father who didn't know him or understand him.

"We lasted a year together. My father was itchy and silent the whole time, stuck in a desk job he hated because he couldn't leave me alone. When I turned sixteen and they couldn't come after me as truant anymore, I split before school started again that January. I got my GED later, did college and the police academy on my own. I hear from my dad once, maybe twice a year. We're not close."

He ran out of steam after that and they sat in silence while Holly turned something over in her mind. She didn't want to discount anything Alex had said tonight, but his story made her wonder about something. She didn't realize she was shivering until Alex pulled the blanket off the sofa bed and tossed it to her.

"I've kept you up way too long, and you're freezing."

She wrapped it around her, grateful for the warmth. "I don't mind being up. But I was cold. Thank you." The fleece blanket over her robe would be too warm soon, but for now it was a comfort.

She didn't know quite how to begin what she wanted to ask Alex. Taking a deep breath, she just plowed ahead. So far that had been his style, and she was beginning to see the utility in it. "Okay, now that I've heard all this I've got a question."

"Sure. I'll answer just about anything. I think I owe you for listening to all this. It was a lot more than I meant to say."

Holly felt like telling him that knowing all this endeared him to her more than she could tell. Alex was human in a way he'd never been before when he was keeping up his tough-guy front as her body-guard. But he'd said he'd answer just about any-thing, and she had to keep going now while he still felt that way.

"I'm not very good at expressing myself. Maybe that's part of why you think I need help." She held up a hand to stop his response. "I only said that might be part of it. But I've been thinking. There can't be too many things more awful than watching your mother disappear in front of you without being able to do anything about it."

"You're right about that one." Alex didn't look as if he knew where this conversation was going. Holly wasn't all that sure she knew herself.

The blanket was getting a little overwarm now, but she didn't want to let go of it yet. Having some-thing to hold on to felt good. "You've said you see your mother in me, a little, and in this apartment you see some of the places you lived. Do you think you might be seeing things that aren't there?" Holly tried to find just the right words, where she could make her feelings known without being hurtful or discounting his pain. "I know you'd give anything to be able to do something for your mother. Do you think that just maybe you might be seeing things with me as more serious than they are?"

His brow furrowed. "So that I could rescue you, the way I couldn't help my mother?" He was silent for a very long time. "I don't know. I don't think so. But maybe it's possible...." He didn't sound convinced of the idea, but Alex sounded less sure of himself than he had in the past hours.

"Is there anything I could do that might make you believe I wasn't as bad off as you think?" She hoped there was. And she hoped it was something simple.

"Maybe. Perhaps something like a real informal second opinion. Is there somebody you could talk to? Your pastor at that church I haven't made it to yet? Anybody?"

It was hard for Holly to think about talking to Reverend Burns about this. He seemed very wise and fatherly, but not terribly approachable. "I don't know. I suppose I could ask about something, anyway."

"Good. I'd feel better if you did. Maybe I could go with you this weekend, get a chance to see some of these folks around town I haven't met yet."

"That would be good. But for now I'm going to have to go on back to bed. Let me give your blanket back. You're the one who looks cold now." She stood up and removed the blanket from her shoulders.

Alex moved the pillows he'd piled at the back of the couch into an arrangement that looked more comfortable for sleeping. "I can't argue. This discussion seems to have worn both of us out. For the first time in a while, I'm having trouble staying awake."

"Gee, should I tuck you in?" Holly tossed the blanket over Alex, still covered by the bedsheets she just realized he'd never removed. She was thankful for that small barrier, because once again the air between them seemed charged, only now it was with an entirely different sort of emotion.

"No, better not tuck me in. Just the offer has me more awake than I want to be right now. Get some rest, Holly. And Sunday we'll go to church and talk to your pastor."

Heading to the bedroom, she didn't bother with the lights, just closed the door behind her and dived into the bed as fast as she could shed her robe and climb between the covers. Even then sleep was a while in coming while everything that Alex had said fought for space in her overcrowded brain.

Chapter Nine

She wasn't going to be able to do it, Alex thought as Holly got nearer and nearer to the door where Reverend Thomas Burns was shaking hands with churchgoers at First Peninsula Church as they made their way into the church basement for coffee fellowship. A few people had somehow come behind Holly and the boys, so he was watching her progress toward the minister. Alex could tell by the set of her shoulders and the tilt of her chin that when she got up there to the older man, she would just say good-morning and pass on through with the rest of the crowd.

The reverend, who looked to be in his early seventies, seemed a kindly man. He appeared to favor one leg, and had made a reference in his sermon this morning to his constant battle to try to stave off knee surgery. He reached down and ruffled first Aidan's hair and then Conor's. Each boy smiled up at him and zoomed off toward the tables that held cups of juice and various cookies and pastries. "Don't get too far ahead," Alex could hear their mother caution. "And remember, one goodie apiece."

Once she got even with the minister, Holly looked back, apparently still expecting Alex to be next to her so that she could make introductions. Alex apologized to the small family between them and stepped up to Holly's side.

"Alex Wilkins. I'm a friend of Holly's," he told the minister. No sense in bringing his job into the church house with him. The man's handshake was friendly, but he didn't have much of a grip. Alex was beginning to wonder if his urging Holly to unburden herself on her pastor was such a great idea. They all three made a brief amount of small talk, and Alex and Holly drifted toward the tables where the boys had selected their cookies and were getting cups of bright red punch.

The cookies were heart shaped, decorated with pink and red sparkly sugar and frostings. Looking at them, Alex realized that it really was February already, and Valentine's Day was coming up soon. He wondered if Holly knew that. "A little early to start celebrating, isn't it?'' he asked, holding up a pink cookie.

Holly rolled her eyes. ''You're kidding me, right? There's only about ten days until Valentine's Day. You couldn't get a table at The Bistro, or any other decent restaurant for fifty miles around if you waited until now. We've been more than half booked for weeks, and the last of the slots between noon and nine in the evening filled up this week.''

So much for her not knowing the holiday was coming up. And so much for any possible celebrating Alex had begun to concoct. He had a sinking feeling about that anyway. ''So, if Valentine's Day is such a big deal at work, I'll bet you're putting in a long shift.''

''It's about the biggest deal of the year for a restaurant like The Bistro. Romance is the name of the game there. Felicity and I will both be putting in five hours at lunch and coming back for five more at dinnertime. The plus side is, the tips are great.'' Her smile was sunny.

''Yeah, and the more we talk about this the less I'll notice that you didn't say anything but good-morning to Reverend Burns, right?'' Alex pointed out.

Holly's smile faded a little. ''I couldn't. Not that I would have said much in that line anyway, besides telling him we needed to talk later. But Alex, I just couldn't. I've got a backup plan, if you can believe it.''

"Great. As long as it's a real plan, let's hear it.'' Alex wondered if he was calling her bluff. He thought he might be, but Holly's smug expression told him otherwise.

She was wagging a finger at him and in the hand that held her coffee cup she was also holding a flyer of some kind by the corner. "You didn't even read your bulletin, did you?''

Alex shrugged. "Not much need for me to see what the Boy Scouts are up to, or who's providing altar flowers next week.''

"Ah, but there's plenty of call for you to know what's going on around town. And if you'd looked, you would have seen there was a reminder for those of us who belong that the Safe Harbor Women's League is meeting on Thursday.''

"Which means what?'' This conversation still felt as if it was in a code he didn't understand.

Holly looked as though she wanted to roll her eyes. "Oh, honestly. I know you haven't paid a lot of attention to what goes on in my life besides work, but there is more to it than just going in to The Bistro and coming back home to fold laundry.''

"I'm glad to hear it. Does this mean that the Women's League is part of that vast life outside your apartment, The Bistro and the Safe Harbor Elementary School PTA?'' Okay, so that was probably going to get her a little riled. It might take her focus off his supposed cluelessness.

Her smile this time looked a little rueful. "So maybe I don't have a huge social life. But the Women's League is one of the best parts of the social life I have. And if anybody would have an idea about what we've talked about, it would be Constance and the rest of the bunch there.''

"Good. So you'll go? And you'll say something?''

"I'll go. And I'll even say something." Her eyes were bright with mischief. "But remember, it is the *Women's* League, so you're going to have to stay home for a change.''

Now it was Alex's turn to feel like rolling his eyes. He'd been taken in. "If you say so. Maybe I could wait outside in the car or something.''

"I don't think so. Maybe if you're really anxious to be close to me, you can go next door to the bed-and-breakfast and help the crew that's doing the last of Annie's painting. That way she could come to the meeting.''

"It's a thought. I'm very handy with things like that.'' Her laughter came very quickly. "Well, I am. Can't you picture me with a paintbrush?''

"Maybe. It's just so much easier to think of you working with your laptop, or even doing some high-powered detective work." At least she had a good opinion of him. Alex decided that maybe he should leave this alone before he got any less flattering descriptions of himself.

"Then you've got a deal. If we need to check with Annie and see if she minds an extra crew member we'll do it. But this way I'll feel better about knowing where you are without being in your way."

"Amazing." Holly was still smiling. "Maybe I should have taken you to church more often. I do believe we actually compromised there, Mr. Wilkins."

"Perhaps the first of many." Alex wasn't so sure about that, but they could both hope, he expected.

There were still a couple inches of snow on the ground when Holly pulled into the parking lot at the lighthouse to attend the Women's League meeting. She sat in her car for a moment, looking at the tall structure in its serenity.

For some odd reason she thought about what it must have been like to be the lighthouse keeper in the days when it was a full-time job. What a faith those men, and probably a few women at times, must have had. They had to be trusting God all the time to be able to guide massive ships up and down the peninsula. Did people have that kind of faith these days? Holly knew she didn't. Maybe Constance did. Maybe even Alex, for all she knew. His car was parked in the lot not far from her own. Annie had been overjoyed to have another painter, and had asked him to start as early as he could this morning.

Thinking about Alex and faith in the same breath overwhelmed Holly, and she got out of the car quickly, hurrying toward those women who provided her pillar of faith. If anybody had any answers to her current dilemma, it would be the Women's League.

Opening the heavy door into the meeting room, she could hear the buzz of their voices. Wendy seemed to be regaling the group with a story about the latest antics of one of her preschoolers. Holly made sure she wasn't tracking snow into the room, and hung her coat on the rack to join the others already lined there.

"Holly," Constance called from the corner near the fireplace. "Come on. We saved you a place, because I knew you'd show up."

They had set up the big quilting rack and Holly groaned inwardly. If she'd remembered that they were going to be finishing the quilt the group was making for Annie's bed-and-breakfast, she might have been even later. She didn't understand how the rest of the women seemed to create such beautiful small stitches with so little effort. Hers always looked clumsy and lopsided, and she wanted to rip out as much as she sewed.

Constance would never let her, pronouncing every effort "just fine" even when Holly knew it wasn't, and she was aware that Constance probably redid some of it herself when she was alone. But Constance was an encouraging person, and she wasn't going to hurt anybody's feelings over stitches on a quilt.

Holly fixed herself a cup of coffee and drank a couple sips with her hands wrapped around the mug to thaw out her fingers. Maybe if she warmed up her hands they'd behave better when she tried to sew. It was worth a try, anyway.

She stood for a moment drinking her coffee and listening to the group chat. "So, are all your permits and such in order with the town?" Constance asked Annie.

"I think so. It's sure a slow process. But it looks like by the time I'm really ready to open, everything will work out. I'm more concerned with whether I'll make my own deadline right now."

"Is there anything we can do to help? Should we be doing things for you instead of planning something else for Valentine's Day?" Wendy looked up from her stitching.

"No, really, I think I'm on track. There's just so many little things to take care of." Annie sighed.

"Every time I've got one thing done, something else pops up to take its place."

"If all your town permits are in place, everything else will fall in line, too," Elizabeth Neal pronounced. Holly sat down next to the opinionated ex-postmistress, where there was an empty chair.

"So in those council meetings you've gone to, have you picked up any good gossip?" Liz's eyes sparkled as she quizzed Annie. "Like what's going on with the old bookstore."

"What *is* going on with that?" Constance chimed in. "It looks like somebody's started work in there for some kind of shop. There's a sign in the window that says Coming Soon...The Quest but I have no idea what that is, do you?"

"Whatever it is, it would fall under new business, and mine didn't," Annie said.

Holly felt puzzled. "This is where living here such a short time gets me confused. I thought this was a new business for you."

Annie smiled. "It is, for me. But the building was a bed-and-breakfast before, a few years back. And nothing much has changed in the way of regulations since the original owners got their business permits."

That explained, everybody went back to their stitching for a while with little interruption. Holly knew she should be bringing up her question about what Alex had told her, but she didn't know how to work it in. She couldn't just blurt out in the middle of the companionably silent room that Alex thought she was mentally ill. She concentrated on the quilt in front of her, listening to the small sounds of the crackling fire and the quilting.

Finally Elizabeth put down her needle and pushed her chair away from the quilting rack. "Well, that's enough of that for a few minutes. I've got to get up and pace or something. I'm going cross-eyed."

Everyone laughed while she got up and stretched luxuriously. Holly hoped that she'd still be able to move that way in forty years or so, marveling at Liz's agility as she rolled her shoulders and tilted her head far over from side to side. "That's working the kinks out," Liz said with a small sigh of satisfaction.

"You're mighty quiet today," she said, looking straight at Holly, whose needle stilled as well. "In fact, you're always mighty quiet. Yet you don't strike me as the shy type, Holly."

"I guess I'm not shy, really. Maybe I like the quiet, though."

"It's good to be quiet sometimes," Constance said, looking over a pair of half glasses she was using to see the stitches. Somehow her pointed gaze made Holly uncomfortable being quiet for a change.

"Alex says maybe I'm too quiet," she said. That

was as close to blurting out her troubles as she was going to get.

"Alex? What have I missed around town by staying at the office?" Gracie Adams piped up from her seat in the opposite corner from Holly.

"If that busy husband of mine would give you more time off, you'd know that Holly has acquired a bodyguard of sorts," Wendy said. Gracie was Dr. Maguire's nurse at the Safe Harbor Family Practice, and with a boss as busy as Gracie's, Holly could see why she wasn't able to make every meeting of the Women's League.

"A bodyguard? That sounds interesting."

Holly wrinkled her nose. "I guess so. It's as inconvenient as it is anything. Alex really believes that there's a man with a gun after me. I'm not as sure as he is. Alex was a good friend of my husband's, though, and I know Kevin trusted his judgment as much as he did any other officer's, so I'm willing to let him watch over me for a while." As she was explaining it all to Gracie, Holly realized that was how she felt about Alex, too. She trusted his judgment as much as she did anyone's. She wondered if Alex knew that.

Gracie's green eyes were wide. "Wow. What else did I miss around here? If it's all that exciting, I'm going to have to come more often." Laughter followed her remark, and Holly felt as if she'd been taken off the hook for the time being.

She could have let the subject drop then, but if she really trusted Alex's judgment, Holly decided, she needed to keep talking. "I said before that Alex thinks I'm too quiet. He really has said more than that. Alex is trying to convince me to see you folks at the family practice, Gracie. He's trying to convince me that I might be depressed."

"Nonsense." Elizabeth Neal's pronouncement was quick and just as sharp as one of her needle thrusts through the quilt batting. "Way too much of that bandied about these days. If you're feeling down you just need to pick yourself up and give yourself a good talking-to. Depression. Hmmmf." Holly could see Gracie press her lips together as if she wanted to say something but wouldn't.

She seemed to exchange looks with Constance, who gave her a quick shake of the head over the table. "That might be putting it a bit strongly, Elizabeth," Constance said. "I don't think depression is such an overstated thing today. It's a real disease and people suffer from it, just like they do anything else."

"Even Christian people," Wendy said firmly. "Robert is always trying to convince clergy members of that. He's trying to set up something where they could work together on a variety of issues, and that's one of them."

Holly felt as if she might have gotten in over her head. "I don't know if Alex is right or anything. But I promised him I'd say something to somebody else, and you all seemed like the logical choice."

Constance reached over and patted her hand, deftly avoiding the needle that Holly still held. "And we're honored that you would take your problems to us. That's what the Women's League is all about."

"Right. Support, prayer and Elizabeth's brownies," Wendy said, a twinkle in her eyes. "And I could use one of those brownies about now, Ms. Neal. You did bring them, didn't you?"

"Of course. I even put in extra nuts. They're high in folic acid, which if I remember is something you need to be concentrating on in your condition," Liz told her.

The buzz of conversation went on around them as they stopped sewing to snack. Holly let herself be swept up in the socializing and let her serious concerns go. She didn't think anybody noticed that she didn't eat much, and she felt good just having talked to someone who cared.

Later when the afternoon was winding down and she was helping Constance clear away coffee mugs, the group founder stopped what she was doing and looked deeply at Holly. "What Liz said before, about depression being nonsense? She's entitled to her opinion, I guess, but I don't share it."

"Oh?" Holly tried to keep her hands from trembling as she gathered up the used napkins and paper plates. "Do you think Alex might be right about me?"

Constance was silent for a moment. "He might be. I don't see enough of you to be sure, my dear. I know it's a problem I battled for quite some time after Joseph disappeared. And I can tell you that what I went through was very, very real."

Somehow it felt good to hear someone Holly looked up to as much as Constance admit such a thing. "I'm sure it was. How did you deal with it?"

"Support from my friends. Prayer. Talking to Reverend Burns. Seeing the doctor, who found a wonderful Christian counselor in the city. Founding this group helped quite a bit because it kept me busy. I suspect prayer and time were the best things for me."

"And you don't feel that way anymore?" It was hard to imagine that Constance, who looked like such a pillar of strength, ever felt depressed or down about anything.

"I don't feel that way constantly. There are still moments. But they're much fewer and further between these days. As I said, having good friends helps.''

''All your friends, I expect,'' Holly said, knowing she wore the ghost of a smile. It was common knowledge around town that Constance was ''seeing'' Charles Creasy, the police chief.

''Perhaps you're right. After a while having a wide variety of friends, including some who happen to be male, begins to feel right. I've noticed that Alex seems to have taken quite a shine to your boys.''

''He has. And he's very good with them. I don't know what they're going to do when he goes back to Chicago.'' For that reason Holly hoped that he'd stay a while. She didn't want to deal with brokenhearted little boys.

''Maybe the three of them could come to our Valentine's Day tea with you. Will you have any time off that day from the restaurant?''

''A little while between lunch and dinner. Not enough time to get the boys, make sure they're dressed properly and get to a fancy tea.''

Constance smiled. ''Then maybe Alex could do his part by picking them up and getting them dressed. That would be a lovely Valentine, wouldn't it?''

''Definitely.'' Holly wasn't sure which explosion would be bigger, the one from the boys when they found out they were going to a dress-up party or Alex's reaction to what she'd just committed him to.

She found herself smiling back at Constance. "This could be fun." So Alex might fume. At least his fuming wouldn't be over safety concerns for a change. What could be safer than high tea with the Women's League? Even Alex wouldn't be able to argue about that part of her new plan.

Chapter Ten

Holly went next door to pick up her paint-spattered companion and tell him what she'd gotten him into now. Alex was surprisingly unpainted, except for a couple spots on his ancient-looking flannel shirt. "So, how was the Women's League? Did you talk about me?" he asked with a grin.

"Of course. Why do you think we don't let you guys in?" Holly could see that he wasn't sure whether to take her seriously or not. It was fun keeping him in suspense, but she couldn't keep it up for long. "Relax. We didn't talk about you that much."

He looked put out. "And that's supposed to be comforting?"

"Hey, we're not gossips by nature. Quite honestly, we don't talk about guys all that much usually.

It's not like it's a high school sleepover. Mostly today we worked on the quilt that's going to go on Annie's wall, right over there.'' She pointed to the main wall of the bed-and-breakfast's front room. "Which looks very nice, by the way."

"Thanks. I can't say I had that much to do with things in here. Mostly I've been in the bedrooms and breakfast room, touching up trim. It's white,'' he said, gesturing to the splotches on his shirtsleeve. "But I guess you figured that out already."

"That or you've aged significantly in the last couple of hours.'' Holly came up to him, working the one streak of dried white paint out of the front lock of his chestnut hair. The action reminded her that Alex had very little gray in his wavy hair so far, even though he was a few years older than she was.

"So, are you done, or will Annie want you to stay any longer?'' She took her hand away from his tempting hair. "I have to go get the boys from school soon."

"And I want to go with you, so let me clean brushes here and I'll meet you at the apartment, okay?"

"Sounds good to me." Only when Holly was already back in the car and driving toward home did she remember the Valentine's Day tea. Maybe it was better to tell him about it when she told the boys, she decided. They weren't going to be thrilled if they realized they'd have to dress up. Maybe Alex could provide some adult motivation. That, or be just as unthrilled as Conor and Aidan to hear he was going to get to wear his dress-up clothes.

Driving home, Holly kept getting the feeling that the same vehicle was behind her, two or three cars back. Was the black SUV really following her, or had she been listening to Alex too much? It was hard not to be followed in a town this small. More than likely it would turn out to be one of her neighbors, she decided, finishing up some afternoon errands and heading to the apartment complex. But when she drove into the complex, the SUV sped up and went straight on the main road, and Holly put any thoughts of anyone following her out of her mind.

Alex got to the apartment with just enough time to change shirts and get back into the car to go pick up the boys from school. It surprised Holly how much everything felt like family once in a while in situations like this. To a casual observer, they might be the mom and dad in the front seat of the car, with the boys piling in the back chattering about their day at school.

"Guess what we made today?" Conor asked the moment he got in the back seat.

Aidan lunged over and punched him on the arm. "You're not supposed to tell. It's a secret, remember?"

"Aidan, no hitting. Secrets or not, there are better ways to talk to your brother. Now, what do you say first?"

Aidan looked out the window and scowled. "Well, it is a secret. And he was going to tell."

Alex leaned over the back seat, oblivious to the fact that traffic behind them was growing impatient with his parking in the school driveway. "Your mom's right, Aidan. Words are better than hitting. What could you have said to Conor? And it better not include any words you're not supposed to say."

Aidan was still silent, rolling his eyes. Conor sniffled once from his corner of the back seat, rubbing his arm. "I bet that means I can't call Aidan a jerk, either. Even though he is a big jerk for hitting me."

"This is disintegrating rapidly," Holly muttered. So much for being the happy family.

Alex turned around to the front seat, conscious that the line of cars behind him was beginning to stretch to lengthy proportions. "I've got an idea. Do either of you guys know pig latin?"

"Alex, nobody younger than us knows pig latin," Holly said, tempted to roll her eyes herself.

"Cool. Then you can be the first ones on your block to learn." He steered the car out of the line of waiting vehicles and headed toward the street. "How about we find a table at the ice cream parlor and hear about the parts of your day we can know about, and I'll start 'eachingtay' you guys 'igpay atinLay'?''

The chortling from the back seat took over where there had been aggravated silence before. Holly knew she was in for a tremendous amount of silliness in the next hour, but it certainly beat hurt feelings and scoldings. And for a change a little bit of ice cream sounded good, too. Maybe the ice cream parlor would be the perfect place to break her news about going to a fancy tea. At least she could probably slip in the information between bites of cookie-dough ice cream and it would go down more easily with everybody.

Alex looked across the table to Holly and wondered, more than ever, if she was losing her mind. Of course, normally when he wondered this, it was in a perfectly serious vein. Today her somewhat-unhinged behavior gave him hope. If she were feeling well enough to commit them all to a tea party, and a formal one at that, she must be all right. However, she must have known nothing about his lack of skill where it came to clothes coordination. Hadn't she noticed that he wore the same basics over and over? He felt as if his years in a uniform had dulled his fashion sense, if he'd ever had any to begin with.

The boys didn't look terribly thrilled with the

prospect of wearing a suit and tie, either. Both of them had squirmed and scowled a bit when the words *Valentine's Day* and *tea* were put so closely together.

"This tea thing. Will there be anything else there besides tea and dressed-up people?" At least Conor wasn't going to mince words. Alex looked over at Aidan and saw mirrored on the boy's face the same discomfort he felt.

Holly laughed. "Of course there will be other stuff. There will be cake and cookies for the kids, and you don't have to drink tea. That's mostly for the grown-ups, anyway. And being part of the 'dressed-up people' as you put it won't be so bad just for a little while."

"It sounds like church without the color book," Aidan said, making Alex laugh before he could catch himself.

"Sorry, I'm with Aidan," he told Holly. "And I don't even get a color book in church."

"You three are impossible. And he doesn't get a color book either, just a children's leaflet. I imagine there will be plenty of things to do like that at the tea. They're talking about having Kit Peters run a little table where anybody who likes can make valentines. Knowing Kit, I'm sure there will be plenty of paint and glitter and fun things there. Even for

someone as hard to entertain as you." She was looking straight at him, not the two boys.

Alex shrugged. He probably was the hardest of
the trio to entertain. Especially at a fancy-dress tea.
Now, had they been planning to be alone on Valentine's Day he could have thought of plenty of
ways to entertain them both. But it didn't look as if
he was going to get a moment alone with Holly that
day.

He tried not to sigh. "If it's that important to you,
we can do it. Can't we, guys?"

"Sure," Conor said. "Making stuff with Kit
sounds like fun, anyway. And cake. I guess I can
handle a shirt that buttons for a little while for that."

Aidan didn't look quite as convinced, but he
wasn't in open mutiny, either. It looked as if he was
going to have to get these guys dressed up for their
special occasion, Alex thought. He wondered if he
had three ties along with him, much less two that
could be tied any way that didn't come down to
these guys' knees. "We might have to go into Green
Bay to the mall or something," he said. "That or
compromise a little on the tie thing."

"As long as you all three look nice, I won't insist
on ties. I'm sure you'll be just as handsome without
them," Holly said. "Now, finish your ice cream before it melts into soup."

Aidan looked up at her in disbelief. "But Mom,

that's the best part!'' All of them laughed at that, and Alex felt a pang at what he would be missing soon when this job was over and he went back to Chicago.

It didn't sound so tempting anymore, going back to his condo. The bed was comfortable and all his stuff was there, but that was about the only draw to going back. Starting his day without a couple of forty-pound bulldozers landing on the bed would be terribly lonely. And eating breakfast alone in his spotless kitchen wouldn't be nearly as pleasant as watching Holly in her awful, ratty robe muddle around her homey kitchen searching for coffee filters.

And then there was the job he'd be going back to. Every day around Safe Harbor made working for the Cook County district attorney less attractive. True, he was good at his job, and it was a worthwhile service to a lot of people. But surely there was a better way to make a living. Maybe there was even one that could be done here in Safe Harbor once this case was over. It was a thought worth keeping, Alex decided, stirring his half-melted ice cream. He could work on that problem in his spare time, when he wasn't dealing with teaching the kids how to tie a Windsor knot or looking for bad guys around every corner.

Probably the best idea was to use that limited

amount of time in prayer. If God had a plan for his life that included staying here in Safe Harbor, Alex was sure he'd find out about it sooner or later. And he knew it would be sooner if he let God handle the details, because the Lord was always better at that sort of thing than he was himself. If over thirty years of living had taught him anything, it was that.

"Now, you're sure you're okay with this?" Holly asked the morning of Valentine's Day as she was getting ready for work. Alex was packing a bag with the boys' dress clothes so that he could pick them up from school and take them to the tea while she finished the lunch shift.

"I think I actually am." He looked surprised by his own admission. "I'm a lot more comfortable with getting the boys and bringing them to the tea than I will be at the tea itself."

"Fancy dress just isn't your thing, huh?" Holly wished he'd said something earlier. Maybe she wouldn't have pushed this if she'd known it would make him that uncomfortable.

"It's not the clothes that will bother me. It's knowing that I can't wear my ankle holster in a room crowded with women and children. Too many chances for disaster. I'll keep the gun in the lockbox in the car, but I don't like the idea."

Holly studied him silently for a while. He looked

so calm and everyday, chestnut hair a little mussed and his flannel shirt open at the collar. It was hard to think of Alex as her alert, police-trained bodyguard while he sat at her kitchen table. "You've been wearing it when you've escorted me at The Bistro, haven't you?"

"Most of the time. I'm just more comfortable knowing I could protect you if I needed to. And I have all the right permits to carry concealed, even outside my jurisdiction like this. I checked with the police chief to make sure. The last thing I needed was an arrest by the guy I need to be my best friend if anything happens."

Holly shuddered. "I'd forgotten about all this. It's been just long enough since Kevin was alive that the constant worrying about someone in danger had almost worn off. I'd definitely forgotten how much I dislike loaded guns."

Alex shrugged. "They're the only kind to have. As long as they're not around little kids or other major safety risks, I'd certainly recommend one. Especially in the situation you're in right now."

"I'm not so sure what kind of situation I'm in, Alex. It's been weeks since that incident with the kid knocking on the door, and you haven't heard anything else that could even prove that Rico's still anywhere near here."

"I haven't heard anything that proves he's left,

either.'' His hazel eyes were narrowed, making him look grim. ''And unless I do, we're going to be cautious. You'll keep looking over your shoulder, and I'll keep wearing the ankle holster.''

''For how long?''

''As long as it takes. That could be days, or it could be weeks or months. We'll just have to see.''

''Gee, I'm so glad I started this cheery discussion.'' Holly felt like marching out of the room so she could finish getting ready for work in peaceful silence. It beat being reminded that she was putting her life on hold while a stranger decided how she spent her days.

''Sorry I'm not able to give you the answers you wanted. But I know you don't want me to lie to you, or even gloss over the truth.''

Holly settled down a bit. ''No, and I appreciate that about you, Alex. It's good to know that you don't hide things from me. Or at least any more than you have to. That's one of those other things I remember from being married to a police officer. I never knew everything that went on in his life.''

Alex crossed the distance between them. ''You may not know everything, but I've told you as much as I possibly could. I hate being left in the dark myself, and I'll never leave you there if I can help it, Holly.'' He was so close that she could reach out and touch him, and his eyes seemed to be asking her to do just that.

Holly felt aggravation flare up in her. Why did Alex always feel the need to take care of her? Didn't he know that she could take care of herself? And why pick now, when they were nearly out the door, to get all solicitous, and maybe even romantic?

Then the incongruity of her thoughts made Holly laugh. "No, honest, I'm not laughing at you," she told the startled Alex, who'd drawn away from her half a pace. "I'm laughing at me. I was getting all tense about you wanting to take care of me, and at the same time making those big eyes at me like you were going to get all mushy on me."

"What better time than Valentine's Day?" Alex said, his smile coming back as he moved closer again.

"See, this is where you're the civilian for a change," Holly told him, even as she let him put his arms around her. "I can't think of a *less* romantic day of the year for people in the restaurant business. Especially working someplace like The Bistro. Everybody will be in high gear all day, rushing around and trying to please all the customers. Jon-Paul will be impossible by two in the afternoon, and a basket case by seven."

"Yeah, that's romantic, all right," Alex said,

leaning his forehead down to touch hers. "No wonder you laughed."

She stayed where she was, enjoying the warmth and the closeness of him for what might be the last time in twelve hours or more. As much as she argued for her independence, Holly had to admit that having a big, strong, affectionate man around was wonderful most of the time. It pointed out just how much she'd missed in the past two years.

"Tomorrow," she said. "We can try to have our own private romantic getaway tomorrow."

"Right. On Saturday, when you'll be doing laundry and the kids will be bouncing out of their bedroom as soon as it gets light to watch cartoons in my bedroom, also known as the living room."

Finally she pulled away, knowing that it was time to go to work and nothing could delay that any longer.

"All right, so it won't be real practical. Maybe we can work something out anyway. I'll see if Brett would be available for a while in the afternoon. We could go to the diner for a late lunch and a walk around downtown afterward if it's not snowing too hard."

"That has possibilities," Alex said, smiling. "Now let's get you to work so we can get shift number one done and get to the fun stuff."

"Sounds like a plan. Let me grab my purse and

I'll be ready to go.'' Holly headed for the bedroom, the skin of her forehead still tingling where their bodies had met.

Hours later in her few free moments at work Holly was still thinking about their encounter in the living room. How could just standing still with someone, talking and barely touching, be so intimate? Catching a glimpse of Alex as he sat in the kitchen, doing little detail tasks for Jon-Paul, made her heart sing. He was here because he cared about her, and she had to admit that she was beginning to care about him, too.

True, her caring was different from what Alex probably felt. She was enjoying having him around, not only as a presence for the boys, but for herself as well. She was fairly sure that this was still just a job for Alex. Maybe it was a very important job, made more important by the promises he might have made on behalf of an old friend. But would he really feel any regret at walking away when this was over?

Holly picked up the plates to go out to the next table of customers, and as she did, Alex looked up and his warm gaze met her look. There was that thrill through her again, and she knew she was grinning at him. It was good to see him smile back. ''I thought I was supposed to be watching you,'' he said softly. No one else was close enough to the two of them to hear his words in the noisy kitchen.

"Maybe I'm just trying to make your job easier," she said, heading toward the dining room. "There's a first for everything, you know."

"And your cooperating and making my job easier would definitely be a first," she heard him say as the door swung shut behind her.

Every trip in and out of the kitchen was like that, bantering back and forth with Alex. Between the constant flow of customers and the ongoing conversations, the lunch shift flew by.

Before Holly knew it, Alex was up and heading for the parking lot to go get the boys. "I'll get them dressed and we'll be over to the meeting room at the lighthouse by three."

"Great. By then I'll be done here and maybe even have time for a cup of tea there. A little chance to put my feet up would be great."

"I'll say," Felicity added as she swung through the kitchen herself. "Seeing you two almost makes me wish I'd signed up for the tea, even if it was just me and Jasmine going."

"You could come," Alex said, hand on the door handle. "I bet they could handle two more."

Felicity shook her head. "Can't. I need to spend the time between shifts at the copy shop and the post office again, anyway."

"More custody stuff?" Holly knew just how much her friend had gone through dealing with Jasmine's father's family.

"Yeah. Another raft of paperwork for our friends in Green Bay."

"Your lawyer doesn't handle all that?" Alex asked.

Felicity shrugged. "She would, if she were closer. But just like the other side, my lawyer's in Green Bay, too."

Alex shook his head. "There's no decent family law firm here in town?"

Holly shook her head. "There's no family law firm here period, good or otherwise. Safe Harbor may be one of the few places in the state that's actually short on lawyers."

"Amazing," Alex said. "And a subject I'd love to discuss a while longer, but I have to get going."

"Yes, you do," Holly agreed. "I've got two tables to wrap up and I'll see you at the lighthouse."

He nodded and was gone, a brief blast of winter air entering the kitchen as he left. It was rather welcome in the atmosphere that had been heated by hours of cooking.

Felicity sat down on a stool for a moment. "I have to take two minutes as a breather. I'm bushed. I only had one less-than-full table the whole lunch shift. I actually felt sorry for the guy. The girl he was expecting never showed, I guess. At least he left a decent tip even though he got let down.''

"I didn't have any disappointed parties. But these two tables will be if I don't get their desserts out there," Holly said, getting everything arranged on her tray. Even on the busiest day she'd had in weeks, she found herself humming happily as she headed to the dining room again. A few more minutes and she could take a real break. Spending that break with her three favorite guys in the world sounded better than anything else she could imagine.

Chapter Eleven

The meeting room at the lighthouse was more crowded than Holly had ever seen it. There were red, white and pink crepe-paper streamers everywhere. Shiny, heart-shaped Valentine decorations were on every wall, and several small tables were scattered around, bright with red cloths and white candles.

"This is great," Holly told Constance, who looked festive in a red sweater and charcoal wool slacks. "Whoever did the decorating really did a good job."

"It was mostly Annie and Kit. I helped some, when I wasn't helping Elizabeth frost cookies and petits fours."

"The guys will be glad they dressed up and

came." Holly looked around the room. "Did they beat me here?"

"Your boys? Who were they coming with?"

"Alex was picking them up from school. I guess he hasn't made it here yet."

"Not yet, but I suspect they'll be here soon. So far it's been mostly people who haven't had schoolkids to pick up, like Wendy and Robert. Theirs are in preschool, and it lets out earlier."

Holly could see the Maguires at one of the corner tables, Robert helping one tiny girl with a plate of something, Wendy balancing a second child on her shrinking lap. She'd already bemoaned to the Women's League that even though she was a little shy of her fourth month, she had gone into maternity clothes.

"Elizabeth and Annie are out in the kitchen getting more trays of tea things set up." Constance motioned to the small kitchenette down the hallway off the main room.

"Great. I'll go give them a hand until my family shows up," Holly said, heading for the little space.

She wasn't really sure a third person would fit in the room that was really little more than a narrow galley. The hallway leading to the kitchen wasn't much narrower than the kitchen space itself. When she got there, Annie waved. "Hi. I heard you out there. Don't you dare try to come in here and help.

You're supposed to be on a break from this kind of stuff, remember? Besides, you need to find your guy, don't you?'' Annie asked.

Now Holly was definitely confused. ''Alex? I didn't think he was here.''

''I didn't see him, but Elizabeth did,'' Annie said.

''Oh?'' Holly wondered where the boys were. She was about to ask, but Elizabeth was already answering.

''Well, there was certainly a good-looking guy asking for you just a minute ago. I expected it was Alex, anyway.'' Elizabeth went back to stacking cookies on her tray.

Holly knew there was no use trying to help the two efficient women in the kitchen, and she wanted to see where Alex could have gotten to, so she went down the short hallway toward the main room. When she was halfway there she heard someone calling her name. She looked in the direction of the main room, but the voice wasn't coming from there. Down the hallway the other way, toward the back door to the building, she heard it again. ''Holly?''

It sounded like Alex. Holly wasn't sure what he could be doing at the back of the building instead of coming through the front door. At least it would explain why Constance hadn't seen him, she thought. Then she wondered if he'd had some problem getting the boys dressed. Alex knew she was expecting them to look their best, and maybe he wanted a little help before going into the party with all her friends. It struck her as kind of sweet in a way.

Holly changed direction and headed down the hallway. "Alex?" she called, opening the door a little wider. "What are you doing out here?"

As she got to the doorway, an arm shot out and grabbed her wrist, pulling her through the half-open door. The cold air shocked her as she struggled to stay on her feet. The hand gripping her was hard and cold, not at all like Alex's caressing touch would have been. She looked up, stunned, as the man pulled her forcefully against the icy wall of the building. "That was easier than I expected." The man's voice was low and harsh.

Holly's wrist hurt where he'd pulled her out of the building, and the back of her head throbbed where she'd struck the wall. But what hurt most of all was the knowledge that she was alone out here, face-to-face with Rico Salazar, and no one knew where she was.

Alex knew he was running late, but Holly could forgive the things that had delayed him, he was sure. The boys were being, well, little boys, squirming and giggly about the dress clothes and having their hair combed and their faces washed.

He hustled them out of the car and toward the building, hoping their dress shirts weren't too rumpled under their parkas.

Warm air and the sounds of a party rushed out as they pulled open the door. It was decorated from floor to ceiling inside, hearts and streamers in every shade of pink and red competing for attention. Alex looked around for Holly, but didn't see her among the crowd in the room.

"Alex?" He heard someone call his name, and wondered who recognized him in here. Felicity surely wasn't here, and he wasn't sure if he knew anyone else in Holly's Women's League group. A dark-haired woman in a red sweater came toward him, smiling.

"Hi, I'm Constance Laughlin. I recognized Holly's boys, and I'm guessing you're Alex Wilkins. Holly will be glad to see that you're all here, and looking so nice," she said, talking to Aidan and Conor for the last little bit before they dashed off to where Annie Simmons was putting down a tray of pink-iced confections.

"I saw her car out front. Where is she?" He looked around the room again, still not seeing Holly.

"She went back to the kitchen to help Annie and Elizabeth," Constance told him. "It's a small room, so she can't have gotten far." She directed him down a hallway at the back of the room, and as he went back to the kitchen he saw Annie picking up another tray.

"Hi, Alex. You two just keep missing each other, don't you?"

A silver-haired woman peeked out of the galley kitchen and her forehead wrinkled when she looked at the two of them. "Did you just call him Alex?"

"Sure," Annie said. "Why, Elizabeth?"

The older lady shook her head. "That wasn't the man I saw. The one asking for Holly. The other man had darker hair and dark eyes."

Alex felt his heart start to race. "There was another man here asking about Holly? How long ago?"

The woman Annie had called Elizabeth reflected. "Maybe ten minutes, fifteen at the most. I thought it was you, and I told Holly that when she came back here. She's back out in the front room, isn't she?"

Now all the alarm bells were ringing in Alex's head. "No, she's not." He looked around, wondering where else Holly could be, and if his worst fears had come true.

There was nothing else down the narrow hallway except two doors at the other end. One, he knew, led to the lighthouse and the bed-and-breakfast and he was fairly sure it was kept locked all the time. It had been locked when he'd been painting in the bed-

and-breakfast, anyway, and Annie had told them that was the way it always was.

He dashed down the narrow hallway to the other doorway and flung it open. It opened into the outdoors, where there was just a narrow strip of ground before a fence outlined the rocky surface of the cliff down to the beach past the lighthouse. "Holly," he called, searching right and left.

"Alex!" Someone screamed his name far to the left and he craned around, looking at the other side of the picket fence. He could see a flash of the white silk blouse Holly had worn with her black server's pants, and her long, dark hair blown by the wind. And worst of all, a large man was dragging her away down the rocky cliff, and he looked a lot like Rico Salazar.

Alex was in a panic. He had at least three things to do at once, and making one mistake could mean that he'd lose Holly right before his eyes. He couldn't go after Rico unarmed, and he had to let somebody else know what was happening. And there were the boys to think about. He couldn't very well dash off and leave them without putting them in someone's charge. Every second counted.

He went back into the hallway, closing the door behind him, and ran to the main room. The prayers he was breathing almost as a reflex must have had their effect, because the first person he saw was

Charles Creasy, still in uniform, with one arm lightly around Constance's shoulders.

"Chief. I hate to break up your party, but we've got big trouble. Holly's been abducted, and I'm pretty sure it's Salazar."

Charles let go of Constance and reflexively checked his holster. "Abducted? From here?"

"Out the back door. I just saw them go down the cliff. What's down there?"

"Not much. A narrow ledge about ten feet down. If he's got a car stashed he could work his way around the point to the other side of the lighthouse. Or if he doesn't..." The chief didn't finish his sentence and Alex's stomach churned as he pictured the rocky lakeshore below the ledge and thought about Holly landing there.

"We've got to hurry. I'm going to go get my gun. It's locked in the safe in the car." He turned to Constance. "Can you watch the boys? I can't just leave them."

She was already nodding and urging Charles toward the door. "I understand. We'll keep them here and make sure they don't know what's going on. But I *will* make sure the adults do know, and that we start praying for all of you right away." Her bright eyes were moist. "You two be careful out there. And bring her back in one piece."

"We will," Alex said, unwilling or unable to consider any other possibility.

"Where are you taking me?" Holly asked, forcing the words through chattering teeth. It was so cold on the narrow ledge that she could hardly draw breath. Rico didn't appear to be afraid of heights, given the speed he was dragging her along.

Her mind was racing through what she should do next. She and Alex hadn't ever talked about this. He had been so sure that if Rico showed up he'd be able to protect her that they hadn't even considered a hostage situation. Holly knew that she was good alive to Rico only if he needed to get away from Safe Harbor. Otherwise it would benefit him more if she were dead.

The thought made her shudder even harder. He still hadn't answered her, but at least they were at the end of the ridge, and heading up a narrow path. It gave her the slightest bit of hope, because the ledge would have been the perfect place to get rid of her. There was a black SUV parked in the dunes, and Holly had a shock of recognition. "You've been following me for days," she said, remembering the vehicle from school.

"Yeah. You're hard to get alone. That boyfriend of yours is something else."

Holly started to tell him that Alex wasn't her boyfriend, but what did it matter? Maybe it was better if he thought that Alex had every reason possible to follow her, not just the need for her as a witness.

Rico stumbled on the rough dunes, and the action loosened his grip on her wrist. Holly used the opportunity to wrench away from him, putting a little distance between them.

"Where are you going to go?" Rico lunged after her. "There's nobody else out here, and I've still got the gun." He pulled an automatic out of one of the pockets of his parka. "It's not like I'll miss at this distance, or I mind shooting you, either."

For all his argument, he didn't fire, and Holly didn't move any closer to him. She stopped trying to run on the rough ground, but she kept several strides between them. She was so cold. Waves of pain washed over her, not just the pain of the freezing cold around her, but pain at thinking that she might never see her boys again, get to hold them. She pictured Alex and the hurt in those hazel eyes if Rico managed to kill her. There were things she needed to tell him, too, and Holly realized she wanted to do so much she hadn't done with her life already.

"Dear God, help me!" she cried out, unaware that she'd shouted the words out loud until she saw Rico's wide-eyed reaction.

"You believe in that stuff?"

"God? Yes, I do." Holly tried to will her shivering to stop so Rico could understand her words.

"Lot of good your God has done you so far. You're raising two kids alone, working a crummy job and driving an old car." Rico's eyes held a challenge, but he seemed to have decided not to shoot her right away.

"Raising my kids alone wasn't God's doing," Holly said, wondering at her words even as she said them. It wasn't the way she would normally have chosen to witness to anybody, but she had the strongest feeling that God was in control here, regardless of what happened to her.

"He sure didn't stop me pulling that trigger. Didn't stop your old man from dying either, even though he was praying in that garage once he saw me."

"Was he? Good. I hoped he had a chance to do that, and now I know. Thank you so much for telling me that." Holly's eyes filled with tears, partly from the stinging wind and partly from the image of Kevin facing his last moments with this same awful man. At least he had died knowing he wasn't alone with him.

Rico's expression was questioning. "You're thanking me? Lady, I killed your husband, and if you don't turn around and get in that car, I'm going to kill you. Why aren't you screaming and going nuts?''

"Because it won't do any good. You'd like it if I begged and pleaded, but it wouldn't stop you from shooting me if you decide to do it.''

"What's to decide? You're the only one who can testify that I'm a cop killer. With you gone, all they've got is a cop shot with an unregistered gun, no prints.'' He motioned toward her with the gun. "But if you get in that car I could delay things. Maybe even change my mind. You'd make good insurance for my trip to Canada. With you along I could make it to the airstrip, no problem. And maybe when we got there, I wouldn't shoot you after all.''

So that was how he was planning to get away. If he was telling her the truth. Holly felt that every second she spent here on the dunes would give Alex a chance to find her. She felt certain that if she got into that vehicle with Salazar, her life wouldn't be worth much.

As if to verify her thoughts, the winding road on the other side of the lighthouse was suddenly filled with vehicles. She could see a Safe Harbor police car, and Alex's car, as well.

"Okay, that's it. Stop messing around and get in the car.'' Rico moved closer as if to grab her wrist again, but it was hard for him to do while keeping the gun trained on her on the uneven ground, and Holly moved away from him as fast as he closed in.

''No. I'm not going anywhere with you,'' she cried. Men were pouring out of the cars that had come to a halt now, and they were shouting at Rico to drop the gun and give up.

The SUV was between them and the police, forming a barrier that would make it hard for anyone to get a shot off at Rico. Holly could see him calculating the odds, and in his indecision she took the chance of breaking into a run away from him. With a snarl he headed after her, and she tried to increase her speed. But her cold muscles and nearly frozen feet weren't cooperating and the dried grass on the dunes tripped her up. Sprawling, she fell flat and as the breath left her, she expected Rico to be on top of her, dragging her to the truck.

''God, help,'' she gasped out again. Rico stumbled, then gave a growl that was almost feral and ran away from her, toward the passenger side of the SUV. In a few strides he reached the vehicle, flung open the door, rolled across the seats and managed to slam the door behind him. In another few seconds the powerful engine roared to life, and as his tires spit sand, Holly, still flat on the cold ground, could hear Alex shouting over the other noise.

''No, hold your fire. Holly's in there with him!'' His anguished words made her aching body move at last. As the SUV's tires gained purchase on the sand and the vehicle started to move, pulling backward at an angle away from the cliff, she stood up and started waving both arms.

"I'm over here. He's alone," she called, sure that her voice was being drowned out by the wind, the engine of Rico's vehicle, everything. But Alex must have heard her, or seen her, because she could hear a cry from him, hoarse, but somehow almost joyful.

"She's okay. She's over there. Holly, hit the dirt. Now."

She faltered for a moment, unsure whether to do what he said or not. Rico could still use the powerful vehicle to run her over, and she'd make an even better target for that if she was down on the ground. Still, Alex had been right so far on everything. She'd gotten in trouble only by ignoring him. So she dived for the cold sand again. As she did, she could hear the "pop" of automatic fire and bullets pinging off the metal of the truck.

There was chaos as Rico tried to turn the vehicle in the unyielding sand, the powerful engine protesting as the tires spun. The men at the makeshift roadblock were shouting now and more shots rang out. A bullet found one of the rear tires, which blew out in a spectacular explosion. At about the same time the driver's-side windows of the truck shattered.

Holly watched in horror as the black SUV careened through the sand. It was heading away from her, but that wasn't going to help Rico. Instead of racing around the roadblock, the SUV, off balance and maybe even driverless, headed over the cliff in a mind-numbing scream of metal.

Chapter Twelve

All Holly could think about was getting back to the boys. She was conscious of Alex and someone else picking her up and checking her over for injuries. She wanted to tell them she was all right, but she was shaking so hard she couldn't do it.

"You're not hurt?" Alex sounded incredulous as he held her at arm's length. "I was sure..."

"I'm okay. Banged up and bruised, but nothing else," Holly managed to choke out.

"Nothing but half-frozen and probably scared to death. Let's see if we can get you back to the tea and get you warmed up. Your friends will be glad to see you in one piece."

Holly looked down at her smudged blouse and skinned hands. "I won't scare the boys, you think?"

"Not really. Just tell them you took a fall. You don't have to tell them all the rest unless you want." Alex called to one of the police officers. "You got a blanket in that cruiser? And could you take her back to the lighthouse?"

The officer nodded and started rummaging in the trunk of his patrol car. Finding a blanket, he brought it over and wrapped it around Holly, who accepted it gratefully. "I can't take you back to the lighthouse, too. You'll have to stay here," he said to Alex, sounding almost apologetic.

"I know the drill," Alex told him. "I've done it myself enough times." He turned to Holly. "Don't go anywhere without me. If the tea breaks up, have Annie take you next door, but don't go any farther, okay?"

Holly didn't feel like going anywhere on her own for quite some time. "Fine," she told him. She let the officer usher her back to the car and they made the two-minute ride back to the parking lot in front of the lighthouse.

She hadn't realized what a stir she'd create simply by walking into the building this time. A cheer went up among the Women's League members and their families, and the women clustered around her, asking questions.

Constance was there in a flash, waving the rest away. "Now, don't crowd her." She looked over at the patrol officer who'd ushered Holly into the building. "Everything is all right out there?"

"Almost everything. It looks like the...uh... perpetrator didn't make it. Everybody else is okay. She's the worst off," he said, nodding at Holly.

Constance looked relieved. "So Charles and Alex..."

"Not a scratch as far as I could tell," Holly said. The warm room felt grand, but at the same time she was getting a little light-headed. "I need to sit down."

"Of course." Constance steered her over to a wing chair and unwrapped the blanket from around her once she sat down. "Now, I know that Robert Maguire is going to insist on looking you over. Can we hold him off until we get some hot, sweet tea in you?"

"That would be great. Both the tea and holding off the good doctor for just a few minutes."

"If you ask me, she needs something stronger than just tea," Elizabeth said from the sidelines. "But Robert would have a conniption if we slipped a bit of brandy in her cup, so we'll leave it at tea."

"Where are the boys?" Holly couldn't see them from her seat in the corner of the crowded room, but she could hear children's voices from some-where.

"We kept them busy with the other children over at Kit's valentine table. Once they got busy with the paint and glitter and markers, they were much less upset about you and Alex being gone." Constance smiled. "Let me get them over here for you while Annie gets you that tea."

Holly sat back in the chair, letting the warmth of the room and the sheer normalcy of it all envelop her. How long would it be before she could take a scene like this for granted? People who cared for her surrounded her, and the room was warm and welcoming. Trembling and tears threatened to overwhelm her, but she tried to stay as calm as possible for the boys' sake.

Annie brought her tea and she sipped it gratefully. The warm liquid was so comforting. She'd had just a little when Constance was back, Aidan and Conor right behind her.

"Alex found you, huh, Mom?" Conor asked, examining her from about four feet away. "Why'd you go out without your coat on?"

"It wasn't very smart, was it? I think it's going to take a while to warm up. Want to come help?" She held out her arms, and was overwhelmed by her two solid sons piling onto her lap. She felt several new bruises as they settled themselves in, but she loved every minute of it. When she thought of how close she'd come to not being able to do this again, the tears were back.

Aidan turned on her lap to look at one of her scratched palms. "I bet that hurts. Did you fall down?"

"I did. Out on the dunes on that scratchy grass."

Aidan nodded. "It looks like when I was playing basketball on the playground at school and Jasmine knocked me over. Did you cry?"

"No, but I think I'm going to now." Holly could feel the tears starting to spill. "I'm okay, guys. But it does hurt."

Conor's hand, which felt a little sticky from the art supplies he'd been working with, patted her cheek. "That's okay. You tell us it's okay to cry when you're hurt. Want to see what we made you?" He didn't wait for an answer, but showed her the slightly lopsided construction-paper heart.

Conor's had "Mom" printed in big letters that had been traced in glue and then heaped with glitter. Aidan's had crayoned hearts in bright colors on a square, decorated with a wild assortment of beads, feathers and a little more glitter for good measure. "They're the most beautiful things I've ever seen," Holly said, trying not to sob. "Except for you two, of course."

Aidan made a noise in his throat. "Mommmmm. We're not beautiful. We're handsome. Guys are handsome. *Girls* are beautiful,'' he pointed out in a tone that said exactly what he thought of being called beautiful.

"I'll keep that in mind," she told him, but in her heart she knew that these two boys were the most beautiful sights on the planet for her right now. Over and over all she could do was thank God for sparing her to be with them again.

Through the haze of tears she was aware that there was someone standing over them. It was Dr. Maguire, and he had a boyish smile for them all. "Can I borrow your mom for just a minute, guys? I promise I won't take her anyplace, but I do need you two to slide off her lap."

Conor did so immediately, but Aidan took his time. He sidled down, giving the doctor a suspicious look. Parking himself as close to Holly's knee as he could without being in the way, he seemed to be telling the doctor, silently, that he was there to protect his mother if she needed it.

"Did you two make anything for Alex? He's going to be back in a minute, too." The boys looked at each other. Aidan still seemed reluctant to move.

"Really, I won't go anywhere without you," Holly told them. "If you want to make another one for Alex, maybe you could cooperate on one."

"I guess," Conor said. "But can I tell Kit to make Aidan not hog the glue?"

"If you can find a nicer way to say it than that, Conor Patrick," his mother admonished. The boys dashed over to the table and she turned her attention to the doctor.

"Don't get up yet," he told her, pulling an ottoman over and sitting on it to put himself at eye level. "I want to look you over just where you are. Anything happen I should be aware of out there?"

"Not in the medical sense. I'm cold and a little shaky, and my hands and knees are skinned up. But nobody shot at me or anything awful." Holly found that it felt good to say all that. She was glad the boys were across the room at Kit's table again. She didn't think she would have been ready to admit those things out loud with them present. As far as that went, she might never be ready to admit those things with them present. Maybe some day when they were taller than she was.

Dr. Maguire examined her palms. "Those are going to sting for a while. Your tetanus shots up to date?"

Holly nodded. "Always. Jon-Paul is a stickler for keeping all our immunizations current." Something dawned on her. "Oh, my gosh! Jon-Paul. He has no idea any of this has happened, and he's going to expect me to come back to work," she said weakly. "I'll bet you're going to veto that, aren't you?"

Dr. Maguire gave her a stern look. "You bet I

am. I don't want you going anyplace besides home tonight, Ms. Douglas, and I don't want you going anywhere tomorrow until you've stopped by my office and let me really check things out. You're too close to suffering from full-fledged shock to suit me as it is. If it weren't for the fact I know you'd refuse, I'd love to keep you overnight at the hospital for observation."

"You're right about that. I wouldn't let you," Holly told him.

"That makes two of us." She didn't know when Alex had come up beside them, but he was there, looking stern. "I don't intend to let her out of my sight for at least twenty-four hours, except when she's taking a bath to warm up and clean out those scratches. And even then, I'm probably going to be sitting right outside the door."

Dr. Maguire stood up facing Alex. "Works for me. And you'll get her to my office tomorrow morning? I'm in half a day on Saturdays most of the time, and we'll clear a space for her. You, too, if you need one."

Alex shook his head. "Not needed. Nothing happened to me that hasn't happened a few times before. Charlie Creasy is the only one who needs to keep track of me for a few days."

"Okay. Then I'll see you in the morning." Dr. Maguire looked back down at Holly. "Go home and get some rest. Take a dose of some kind of over-the-counter pain medication, because I can already tell you that you're going to wake up a little sore tomorrow. And come see me before noon.''

''I will,'' Holly promised. ''In fact, once the boys are done with their artwork, I'm ready to go home whenever they are.''

''Good,'' Alex said. ''Because I'm sure ready to take you there. I already called Jon-Paul and he knows everything that he hadn't already seen out the windows of The Bistro. Apparently Rico's plunge could be seen for a mile or so down the lakeshore.''

Holly shivered, remembering the scene. ''I imagine it could. Let's round up the boys and go home, Alex. I need that hot bath, even with you parking yourself outside the door.''

His expression was still grim. ''If I thought you wouldn't argue, I wouldn't even let you get that far away from me. But I know your argument skills, and I expect even this hasn't stopped them totally.'' He grasped her arm gently. ''Let's go get the boys and go home.''

It sounded like the best idea Holly had heard in quite some time.

''Harbor Pizza is making heart-shaped pies for two dollars more,'' Alex called to Holly through the bathroom door. "I popped for the extra, so don't argue, okay?"

"All right." Her reply was just loud enough to be heard over the running water. "How many did you get?"

"Two," Alex shouted back. "One plain cheese and one pepperoni." He was trying as hard as possible to inject some normalcy back in this day. It probably wouldn't work, but he could try, for the boys' sake. They were settled into the living room watching the video that Brett had lent them after they came home. It seemed that half of Safe Harbor had heard about the events of the afternoon and everyone wanted to do something to help.

"Thank you," Holly called back. She sounded so worn out that Alex wanted to pound on the door to insist she keep her head above water in the tub. But he knew how well that would go over, even today, so he kept his mouth shut. He'd already nagged her into taking the pain medication the doctor had recommended, and ushered her in to get her bath and thaw out. For the rest of the night he might as well stick to what he did well, like ordering pizza.

The water stopped running and Alex sat down in the hallway. He hadn't been joking when he'd told Holly that he didn't want to let her out of his sight. Everything that had happened today made him feel like the world's biggest failure. One or two more wrong moves on his part and she could have been dead by now. That made his hands shake just thinking about it.

How had he ever let her talk him into the mess that had led to today, anyway? He had come here for one purpose, and that was keeping Holly safe. Instead he'd let his own feelings, and his willingness to please her, get in the way of his job. And it could have cost them all big time.

Doing his job right would have meant that Rico would never have had a chance at Holly. It would also mean that the guy would still have been alive to put back into custody. Instead it had all gone wrong, and now he and Charles Creasy might both find themselves on some kind of administrative leave while their various departments sorted through who was responsible for Salazar's death.

Alex had used his gun in the line of duty before, but he'd never killed anybody. Never even done more than grazed someone, for that matter. It would be days before the county medical examiner could tell them who'd been responsible for the shot that had ultimately caused this death. But until he heard differently, Alex figured it was his fault, like most of the other disasters today. He leaned against the wall of the hallway, listening to Holly thaw out in her hot bath. At least he could take care of her for the rest of the day. Maybe he could get that much right, anyway.

He wondered if she would be asking him to leave tonight. After all, the job he had come to do was done. There was no reason to believe that anybody else would be after Holly Douglas at this point. Not when there was no longer a suspect to put on trial for her husband's death. Her use as a witness was over.

For that matter, Alex figured Cook County would probably be calling him back to his regular work as soon as possible. They'd have to wait a few days for the medical reports on Salazar, because policy said Alex wasn't going anywhere until the initial investigation into Rico's death was complete. But once that was over with, there would be no reason for him to hang around Safe Harbor. Given the bang-up job he'd done today, nobody would be asking him to stay, either.

Alex could hear around him the quiet, normal sounds of a family settling down for the evening. The video played in the living room, and something on the screen made the boys laugh. Little kids had such great laughs. Conor and Aidan had wedged their way into his heart in such a short time. And then there was Holly. She'd become such a big part of his life in so many ways. This wasn't supposed to happen. This was all supposed to be a job, period.

One he could walk away from with no regrets when it was over. Well, now it was over and just about all he had was a huge pile of regrets.

On the other side of the wall Alex could hear Holly adding more hot water to the tub. "Can I get you anything in there?" he called.

"Nope. Nothing yet. Now, once I'm dried off and dressed in my sweats I'll let you put that charming cream Dr. Maguire recommended all over my hands."

"Don't forget to do your knees while they're still uncovered," Alex told her. "I saw at least one of the dives you took and that kind of thing really makes road rash."

The doorbell rang and Alex could hear the boys calling for him. At least they didn't start opening it on their own. "Be right back," he told Holly through the closed door, reaching for his wallet. He hoped he had enough cash for the pizzas. It would be just his luck that he'd mess up the one thing he was sure he could do right today.

He fished out the wallet, and saw there were several twenties in it. At least one thing would go right in this long, miserable day. Alex got to the front door and looked out the peephole. There was a skinny kid in a Harbor Pizza uniform balancing boxes on the other side of the door.

Alex found himself really looking hard at the kid

before he realized that he was just a young man delivering pizza. There was no reason to think he was anything else this time. No miracle in that, but for a change something was happening the right way. Alex opened the door to get the pizza, wondering if maybe the sheer normalcy of it might be a small miracle in itself.

If so, it was the first one he'd seen all day, and he decided to be grateful for it. The kid probably wondered why he got such a great tip for just delivering two pizzas, Alex thought, but he decided to let him wonder. For somebody out there, this day ought to be remembered as a holiday, and a pleasant time. He closed the door and locked it while holding the pizza boxes in one hand. Juggling them into the kitchen, he went to look for plates and cups and all the things he'd need to set out supper for everyone.

He wondered which one of them would be able to say grace over the food tonight. And what on earth could either of them say that could convey to God all they were thankful for? Maybe it was a day to let Aidan and Conor give thanks over the meal. Alex was pretty sure the Lord would understand.

Chapter Thirteen

The first thing Holly thought when she got out of bed on Saturday morning was that Dr. Maguire had been kind in warning her she'd probably be "a little sore." She felt as if she'd been run over by a steamroller. It was probably a very good thing that she was seeing the doctor this morning. She hobbled over to the mirror to see if her reflection greeted her was as charming as she expected. She wasn't disappointed.

"Ugh," she said to the vision in the glass. She wondered who would have the best comment on her appearance, Alex or the children. Alex would be more succinct, she decided, while the kids would be painfully honest. They had a lot to work with. She didn't know when she'd ever looked like this, even in the days following Kevin's death.

A hot shower perked her up a little, and made the soreness a bit less noticeable. And surprisingly nobody said much at breakfast about how she looked. She had an idea that Alex and the boys had perhaps had a little chat before she came out of the bedroom.

"I took the liberty of calling Dr. Maguire's office once I heard you up and showering," Alex told her as she was rinsing cereal bowls afterward. "He can see us any time after nine-thirty that you're ready to go. And Brett can come up and watch the boys, so we don't have to take them along unless you want to."

"Most places I'd like to take them today, but the doctor's office isn't one of them. Right in the middle of flu season like this, we don't need to add the worry of anybody catching anything nasty," Holly told him. "Besides, Aidan especially hates the doctor's office. He has a real vivid memory of booster shots."

"I have those memories myself," Alex said with a grimace. "So how soon should I tell Brett to be here?"

Holly looked at her watch, surprised how much of the morning was gone already. "Give me ten minutes to try and do something with my hair and I can be ready to go."

Alex nodded and went to the phone while she got ready to see Dr. Maguire.

When they got to the office, she was just as glad they'd left the kids at home. Her prediction of lots of flu sufferers at the family practice was accurate. The stern expression on Alex's face seemed to keep the folks who were discussing yesterday's events from asking them any direct questions. Today that felt like a blessing.

They didn't sit in the waiting room long before the nurse called her name. She expected Alex to insist on going in with her, and was surprised when he waved her into the office while he sat with the same sports magazine he'd been staring at for ten minutes.

If she'd expected to surprise Dr. Maguire with the way she looked, Holly was disappointed. He did suggest a heavy-duty antibiotic cream for the scrapes on her hands, and wrote out a prescription for it. "Now, what else can I do for you?" he asked, sitting down on the stool in the corner of the room near the examining table.

Holly took a deep breath and looked straight at the doctor. This was the scary part, but after yesterday she wasn't about to turn back. "I needed to make an appointment with you before yesterday, but I'd been holding off. Some of my friends have suggested that I might be depressed."

"And what do you think?" His eyes were bright with interest.

"I think they're right. After yesterday, I pretty much know they're right. Out on those dunes with…that man…I realized that life had felt pretty flat for a while. And I wanted to live through whatever happened out there so that I could change things."

"That's quite a revelation," Dr. Maguire told her. "Now let's discuss exactly what makes you believe that, and what we can do about it, shall we?"

Holly could feel her tight muscles relax. So it really was as simple as that? "I think I'd like that. Please forgive me if I get all teary on you."

Maguire waved his hand. "Don't even apologize for it. Remember, I've got two small daughters and an expectant wife. Tears don't bother me, especially the kind that might be called for. So you might be weepy at times. What else is there?"

Holly recited her problems, and once in a while Robert Maguire interjected questions of his own. The more they talked, the easier it became to admit all this to someone. The fact that he was a doctor and a Christian and yet he had no judgment on her made things easier.

"Forgive me for asking this question, because it's going to show my ignorance," he said after twenty minutes of discussion. "I know you belong to the Women's League with Wendy, but I have no idea where you go to church or if you do. Is there somewhere for you to get help with the spiritual side of this problem, as well?''

Holly nodded. ''I wouldn't feel bad about not seeing me at First Peninsula. We don't go to the same services very often, and it seems that when I do see Wendy there, it's always the weekends that you're on call. But yes, I can get help there, as well. I'm even thinking that should be my next stop.''

''It couldn't hurt,'' Maguire told her. ''If you can stand one more set of needles, there is some blood work I'll need to do to rule out some other medical reasons for your depression. But given what you've told me, it sounds like a chemical imbalance made worse by the stresses you've suffered. I hope it will respond to treatment fairly quickly. Most do.''

''I'm glad to hear that,'' Holly told him. ''And as long as I get a really cool bandage to show the boys, even the blood work won't be a problem.'' The doctor seemed to know exactly what she meant. He walked her down the hall to the in-house lab and instructed the young woman there to give her the coolest bandage they had after her blood drawing.

So that was how Holly came to be sporting what looked like a tie-dyed rainbow tattoo on the inside of her elbow when she came out to meet Alex again. She was shuffling paperwork and prescription orders into her purse as she came through the door. Alex looked up when she walked through the doorway, and Holly could tell that each opening of that door in the past half hour had put the same alert look on his face.

He seemed to relax visibly when he saw that it was truly her walking through the door this time. Holly felt touched that just seeing her could do that for somebody. "You're okay? And ready to go?" he asked.

"Yes to both counts. I'll need to stop by the pharmacy on the way home. And I'd like to make one other stop if you have the time."

"Sure. Anything." Alex got up and handed Holly her coat off the rack on the wall. "Just bundle up good, because it's still plenty cold out there."

"You, too," she reminded him, looking back at the rack where his parka still hung. "We don't need either of us getting sick right now."

Alex opened his mouth to say something, then must have changed his mind, because he stayed silent. He stayed that way, too, through their trip to the pharmacy, and didn't argue at all when Holly told him that her next destination was the church.

Once they were at First Peninsula, she had to convince Alex that it would be a bad idea if he stayed in the car in the parking lot. "I know Reverend Burns doesn't bite. You can come in and sit in the library, or out in the main office or wherever you like. But you're coming in."

He shrugged and slid out of the car seat. "You're the boss." He didn't argue about anything, even to point out that Reverend Burns could be out of the office. Holly had been ready to explain the minister's habit of polishing his sermon in the quiet of the empty church on Saturday, but she didn't need the explanation. Which parts of their ordeal in the past twenty-four hours had made Alex this unexpectedly cooperative? And how did she bring back the man she'd been getting to know?

Alex felt caged. The outer office of the church was empty, since it was Saturday. If there had been a secretary there, Alex knew she would have been staring at him by now. He just couldn't sit still. The prints and hand-stitched sampler on the wall were pretty, and probably very soothing, but they didn't do anything for him. Holly was still in the office with Thomas Burns, the door cracked open for propriety. They'd been talking for a while, and Alex couldn't imagine how much more they had to say to each other, especially when Holly had been so reluctant to talk to the man a few days before.

He couldn't pace this small space anymore, and he couldn't sit still. There were several hallways he could go up and down outside this office, and it was time to extend his pacing. Alex went to the door to tell Holly where he would be. His knock roused the reverend from whatever he was saying, and the silver-haired gent got out of the wing chair behind his desk and came over to the door.

"I hear we have much to be thankful for in your presence, Alex," Thomas Burns said to him, his hand extended. "I don't know what you were coming to the door for, but I hope you won't mind if I use the opportunity to thank you."

Alex took the man's hand, fighting the urge to blurt out what he really felt about the past couple days. Holly had obviously glossed things over for her pastor, and he wasn't going to say something different. "You're welcome, but really, I just came over to tell Holly I needed to roam the halls for a while."

Reverend Burns's wide brow wrinkled more than normal. "I was hoping to get a chance to talk to you along with Holly. Are you sure you can't come in for a moment?"

Alex looked over at where Holly was sitting, hoping she'd let him off the hook. Instead her eyes seemed to be asking him to back her up. "For a minute or two, I guess. Although I don't know what good I'll be, in any case."

Reverend Burns went back to his desk chair, wincing a little as he sat down. "These dratted knees. Perhaps they're my thorn in the flesh, as St. Paul says. It's certainly distracting. Your young lady here was pointing out some of my other limitations to me, Mr. Wilkins. Although I know that wasn't her intention in coming here,'' Reverend Burns said, quelling a protest from Holly.

"It certainly wasn't. It's more my own faults that I was pouring out. Especially the fact that I should have brought this problem to your attention weeks ago, when Alex first tried to convince me of it."

Alex looked at her. She was sitting back in her chair, surprisingly calm. There was a tissue clutched in one hand, but it wasn't shredded and it didn't even appear to have been used to wipe away many tears.

"I'm glad you feel that way, Holly. I'm not sure how much help I would have been even a few weeks earlier. It has become clear to me lately that perhaps I could do with a little help around here, primarily where the younger women and children of this congregation are concerned. I suspect that someone with the right kind of training might have picked up your depression simply by interacting with you." Thomas sighed. "Meanwhile, this old man was buried in his books and preoccupied with sixteenth-century organ motets for the upcoming Easter season."

"Please, don't be so hard on yourself," Holly said. "I've been in such denial over this that it wasn't likely to show for any casual observer. It

took Alex nearly living on top of me to point it out
and make me admit I might have a problem.''

She was smiling faintly and Alex couldn't say
anything that would erase that smile. He felt like
anything but the hero that she was making him out
to be. ''I may have overstated the case a little. So
don't put yourself down for not noticing something
that might not have been there.''

''It was there, Alex,'' Holly said, covering his
hand with hers. ''I'm sorry it took so long for me
to admit it. But out on that cliff with Rico so many
things were clear. I knew that my life hadn't been
what I wanted it to be lately. And I knew that if I
got a chance to change that, I'd do it right away.''
Now she had to use that tissue grasped in her other
hand. Alex still felt like the world's biggest heel.

If he'd done his job right, she never would have
been out on that cliff with Salazar. He was ready to
say just that when she got a strange look on her face.
''What?'' he asked. That look didn't have anything
to do with the subject at hand; he finally knew Holly
well enough to decide that.

''The airstrip. I didn't tell you about what he said
about the airstrip. Before you...''

''Killed him,'' Alex finished for her.

''Somebody did. You don't know for certain
whether it was you,'' Holly said, as if that made any
difference. ''Anyway, he told me there were people

waiting for him at an airstrip. That he was getting to Canada that way and if I got in the vehicle with him he might not shoot me there."

She had a wry look on her face. "None of this probably helps today. It would have yesterday if I'd remembered to tell you."

"You had a few other things on your mind, Holly." Alex was surprised at how gentle he could sound.

"This is all fascinating. I've never seen how police business works before," Reverend Burns said. "Do you need to go make some calls or something now?"

Alex hated to burst his balloon. "No, not really. Salazar had a cell phone on him, and there was enough left of it to trace the numbers he'd called recently, and those that had called him. At least now we know where those calls were coming from. The guys who were waiting for him would be long gone by now. And it's pretty much out of my hands anyway."

"Into God's hands," the reverend intoned. "A better place for the whole matter to be, don't you think?"

"Definitely." Alex agreed with him. God wouldn't mess up the whole situation the way he had. He turned to Holly. "Now, do you mind if I go out and pace the halls? I can't sit still very long right now."

She gave him that tremulous smile again that almost broke his heart. "Go ahead. I'll be out soon. I just want to ask Reverend Burns to pray with me, and to recommend a good Christian counselor somewhere. I know that might be a distance."

"Good, because it will be, at least for the present. I'm hoping we can do something to change that situation relatively soon. If you can wait a month or so, I might have good news in that arena." Reverend Burns stood up when Alex did. "And regardless of what you think, I still want to thank you, young man. You've done several good things here. I'm sorry doing them makes you this restless."

He shook Alex's hand again, and for once Alex had no reply. "Restless" was a great way to describe how he felt right now, and even the reverend's compassion did nothing to make the feeling go away. He really needed to roam some more open space right now to burn off some steam.

Holly really thought that her conversation with Reverend Burns, and bringing Alex into it, would have made for long discussions once they got home. Instead Alex basically clammed up for the rest of the day. He even excused himself and left the apartment to confer with Charles Creasy for a couple hours.

"Are you sick?" Aidan asked her while she lay on the couch, an afghan draped over her. Alex was gone and she had quieted the boys into playing with their building toys, which were heaped all over the living-room floor.

"Not exactly. Just very tired," Holly told him. "The medicine the doctor gave me makes me a little sleepy, and I didn't sleep very well last night either, so I think I just need a nap."

Conor came over to join his brother. "You can take a nap. We'll watch you, like you watch us. We won't even drive our cars on the couch." His earnest pronouncement made her laugh.

"That's very sweet. And I think I'll hold you to it. The couch is now officially a toll road. Any cars driving up here, the drivers get a big kiss from Mom."

Aidan rolled his eyes. "Oh, boy. Kissing." He went back to his cars and his brother followed. Holly watched them play, savoring the sweetness of being here at all, and having another day with her boys. She had so much to thank God for, especially sending Alex her way. Without him she might be dead. At best, even if there had been no escape by Rico Salazar, she'd still be in the pit of the despair that had gripped her for so long. Instead she was alive, and on the way to getting better, getting help.

Holly dozed and watched the boys for part of an hour before she heard someone knocking on the door. "It's me, but my hands are full," she heard Alex call. "Open up, somebody."

Holly got up off the couch and went to the door, where out of habit she checked the peephole. It really was Alex on the other side, and he was laden down with grocery bags. She opened the door and he hurried in. "Hope you didn't start dinner, because I stopped and got stuff from the store. We've got rotisserie chicken, a salad, a hot loaf of French bread, the works," he said, sounding more cheerful than she'd heard him all day.

"Great. Can I at least set the table while you get things ready to serve?"

"I guess I'll let you do that." He took the food into the kitchen, and Holly felt as if they'd fallen back into their old companionable ways. Dinner went well, and the meal was over before Holly realized that Alex had said very little again. He was at the countertop, loading the dishwasher while she sat sipping coffee. He looked over and their eyes met, and suddenly Holly knew as plainly as if he'd said it already what was happening.

"You're leaving, aren't you?" Alex looked surprised at her words.

"With Salazar dead, there won't be any trial for you to testify at. His buddies will be more interested in pretending they never knew him than saving his reputation, if he had one. So you're in the clear."

"What about you?" Holly figured she knew the answer to that question already, but she had to ask. "Don't Chief Creasy and the federal authorities want you to stay a while?"

"The county medical examiner says I can go back to Chicago as long as I sign in at work with the district attorney's office and don't go anywhere else until the investigation is over." His eyes glittered the same way hers did, and he swallowed hard. "I'm going Monday morning."

The sounds of Conor and Aidan playing in the next room made Holly's heart ache. "You're telling the boys yourself," she said to Alex. "I'm not doing it for you."

He was by her side now. "Will you at least stay in the room?"

"Of course. You can expect a lot of anger, once they understand what you're saying. And maybe some tears, though probably not from Aidan, not while you're watching."

"I hope they aren't too upset if I shed some myself. I have to do this, Holly, but it isn't easy." His hazel eyes told the story of his pain, but also his relief at admitting all this.

"It won't get any easier," she said, turning away so he didn't see her cry. That upset him, and Alex didn't need any more to upset him right now. He was hurting enough already and she didn't want to make things any worse.

Chapter Fourteen

Sunday was painful for everybody. Holly was still achy and slow from the aftereffects of Friday. They stayed home from church because Holly wasn't quite ready to deal with the attention she knew she'd get from her friends. She felt sure that, put face-to-face with Constance or any of the others, she'd only start crying about Alex leaving. Here with him and the children she could keep her tears at bay.

It wasn't easy, especially in the early afternoon when she was midway through baking a batch of chocolate chip cookies and she heard Alex call the boys to him. She knew what he was doing and didn't know who to feel worse for, him or the boys. If he felt this strongly that it was time for him to go back to Chicago, there was no sense in delaying things.

Holly was a little confused, because she'd thought that maybe they were building something that would last past the end of their business relationship.

When Alex had first gotten here, she'd wanted nothing but to have him gone as soon as possible. But now things were very different. And now it appeared that he was the one who wanted to be gone. Holly had no idea how to ask him to stay instead. She didn't really have the right, when it came down to it. Besides, how could she even consider asking a single, relatively well-off guy like Alex to think about giving up a life he loved for what she had in Safe Harbor?

In the living room she could hear Conor's voice rising. "Leaving? Going away? You mean only for a little while, right? You'll be back when you take care of the bad-guy stuff, right?"

Holly went into the living room, where Alex was sitting on the floor near the boys. Conor was standing, arms crossed over his chest, looking angry and confused. "Mom, make him say something. Alex says he's going away. I don't want him to go away."

"I know you don't, Conor. But sometimes people have to go away." She sank down on the couch, watching the three of them.

Alex seemed to be struggling for the right words. Conor still looked mad, and Aidan was sitting where he had been playing with his metal cars again. He was quiet and looked stunned. He didn't say anything, but looked at Alex hard, expecting something from him. Holly ached for all of them, and for herself at the same time. Tomorrow Alex would be gone, and she would be dealing with two hurt little boys again. It felt very painful and familiar.

"I can't tell you when I'll be back, Conor. It won't be right away. I came here to help your mom out, and I'm done. I have a job to do back where I live, in Chicago. Now that I'm not helping your mom anymore, I have to go home."

Conor had come closer to Alex now. He was close to tears. "Why? You can stay with us. You've got a bed and clothes and a car. Mom cooks good and she takes care of you just like she takes care of us, right?"

Alex turned to look at her, and his eyes were as full as Conor's. Holly knew he wanted her to say something, but before she could, Aidan beat her to it. "He can stay, can't he, Mom?" Aidan blurted out. He came to stand next to his brother. "Say he can."

"It's not that simple, Aidan. Alex is a grown-up. He makes his own decisions on where he goes and when he goes there. Even if I say he can stay, he still needs to be back in Chicago."

"It's not fair. It's not fair at all!" Aidan stormed

out of the room, and they all heard his bedroom door slam. Holly sat in surprise that it was her quiet Aidan who'd had the first outburst and ended up in tears.

She leaned toward Conor as if to draw him into a hug and try to explain things more. But he stepped backward instead and headed toward the bedroom. "I gotta go see Aidan. He needs me."

"They need each other," Holly said softly, as much to explain it to Alex as anything. "That's the one blessing about having twin boys. They understand each other the way no one else ever will."

"Should we follow them?" Alex leaned against her legs, looking up at her for guidance.

"In a little while. Let them deal with this together for a few minutes. Aidan hates to have anybody see him cry or look anything but supertough. Give him a few minutes first."

"Okay." Alex sighed heavily. "This is harder than I thought it would be. This parenting thing never ends, does it? And it doesn't get easier."

"Not that I've seen so far. And my friends with teens say this is the fun part." Holly couldn't imagine how things would get any less fun than they were right now.

Monday morning almost made Alex change his mind. Holly was trying hard to hold back tears, and the boys insisted they weren't going to school. He figured out that one pretty quickly. "I'm leaving whether you go to school or not, guys. I know I told you that when you got home from school today I'd be gone. But if you don't go to school, I'll still leave by ten this morning and you'll miss school."

The boys looked at each other and Alex could see their resolve deflate. "Guess we'll go, then," Conor said, speaking for both of them.

"I'll drive you there. And I want hugs goodbye before we get in the car, because I know there's no way I'd get one at school." Their looks told him he'd got that one right, too.

All too soon they were putting on jackets and loading up book bags. "I'll come back and load up the car," he told Holly, who nodded silently. None of this leaving business was going as smoothly as he wanted it to. Holly wasn't begging him to stay either, so he couldn't exactly back down now. He bent to get his hugs, and two solid little bodies plowed into him. How could he give this up? His throat tightened into a massive ache.

The car ride to school wasn't much better. Aidan surprised him by being the talkative one. "Tell me again why you have to leave. I still don't get it."

Alex suddenly wished quite fervently that he'd insisted Holly come along for the ride. He knew he was going to do a lousy job explaining this to a five-year-old, especially when he was so muddled in his thinking himself.

"Well, Aidan, it's like this," he began, to give himself time. He was praying for help, but no help came in the short span of time that he had to answer the boys. "You know when you promise somebody something, it's good to keep your promise, right?"

"Right," Aidan agreed, but Alex could tell that this wasn't making any sense to him yet.

"Well, I promise to do my job every day, just like your mom does hers, and like you guys are supposed to go to school and do your work. While I was here, my job was taking care of your mom. But I've got another job to do back in Chicago now and they expect me to do it."

"Can't you just keep doing this one?"

"No, this one is over. There's no more bad guys that could be after your mom, but back in Chicago there's still more bad guys for me to catch."

"Don't you want to stay here?" Aidan sounded plaintive.

"Yeah, I do. Staying here would be more fun. But I've really got to take the high ground on this one, guys." They were at school now, and Alex had put the car in Park on the driveway and leaned over the seat to talk to them. "Does that make any sense to you?"

Conor shrugged. "I guess. You never did say when you were coming back."

"When I can. Before summer vacation, okay?"

Aidan's eyes widened. "I hope so. That's, like, forever."

"Maybe to you it is. To me it's just a couple months. For a grown-up that's not forever." Unless you get too tangled up in what you're doing, Alex thought. Then a couple months, like the less than two he'd spent here in Safe Harbor, could feel like forever. "Well, get on in there. Be good, and take care of your mom for me, okay?"

"We do. All the time," Conor said. "Bye, Alex."

Aidan echoed him, and they both slid across the back seat and out of Alex's car while he was saying goodbye. He stayed in the car-pool lane as long as he dared, until they were inside the school and he had no reason not to head back to the apartment.

There he found all his things waiting for him, packed in his suitcase as he'd left them, along with his laptop in its case and another briefcase full of papers tidily arranged. "I told the boys I'd be back before summer vacation."

"Then you better plan on it, mister, because they'll hold you to it. And I'm the one who'll hear about it every day." Alex could tell that Holly was trying to keep her spirits up. *Ask me to stay. Just tell me you need me,* he willed her silently, but it didn't do any good.

"Want to help me carry stuff down to the car?" It wasn't a romantic goodbye.

"Sure. Let me put on a jacket and grab my keys. You've gotten me in the habit of locking up after myself now. No reason to lose it, I guess."

Together it took them only one trip. Once the trunk and the back seat were loaded there was really no reason to go back to the apartment. "Well. I guess this is it." Now that the moment was here, all Alex could think about was some way to delay his departure.

"Did you want a cup of coffee for the road? I made a fresh pot while you were gone, and thanks to you there are two travel mugs in the cabinet."

"Sure. I was going to stop at the diner, but this would be better." He followed her upstairs one last time, wondering why he had been so sure leaving was a good idea.

Watching Holly unlock her apartment, go into the kitchen and fix him a cup of coffee reminded him why he was leaving. Here was a beautiful, strong, independent woman. She didn't need his help anymore, and he'd almost gotten her killed. It was time to let her get back to a normal life.

She put the lid on the mug after pouring in just a little milk, the way he liked it. "You'll call me once you get back home? There aren't supposed to be storms between here and there, but you never know this time of year.''

"True. Sure, I'll call you." He took the mug from her, only to set it back down on the kitchen table. "Now come tell me goodbye."

It was better here in the kitchen instead of out in the parking lot where all the neighbors could see their last goodbye. Here Holly felt free to walk into his arms, where he gathered her in for one last embrace. How could he abandon such kissable lips? Her dark hair felt like silk through his fingers and her skin under his touch was velvet. Long moments passed as he tried to memorize every bit of her.

Finally he had to pull away or lose his resolve altogether, so he pulled away. "You call me, too, okay?"

Her violet eyes glittered. "I will. Stay safe out there, you hear me?"

"I hear you. Goodbye, Holly." He picked up his coffee and headed to the front door while he still had the nerve.

"Goodbye." Her voice caught a little, but she didn't plead, didn't cry. Then the door was closed behind him and Alex heard the lock turn as he walked away. It sounded like finality.

Holly got through Monday, although she wasn't sure how. Tuesday she and the boys were all grouchy at the breakfast table, to no one's surprise. By ten that morning she'd done everything she could do around the house and was going stir-crazy, so she called The Bistro. "Tell me you expect a busy day and you need extra help," she said.

He laughed. "No such luck. You're not scheduled to work until Friday, so don't try coming in sooner. I always give at least a week's vacation to anyone who's been shot at. Alex would have my hide if he found out I'd let you come back any earlier. He came by here yesterday morning and said goodbye and made me swear to take care of you. Chicago isn't far enough that he won't check up on me."

"If you say so."

Holly hung up the phone and glared it at. What was she going to do for three days? Things got even worse when she picked the boys up from school and started sifting through the papers they'd brought home.

"When did they schedule an all-school teacher work day tomorrow? I don't remember that one." Now she had not only herself to entertain, but the children, as well. In the mood she was in that would be a challenge.

"We can do something fun. Maybe Alex will take us…" Conor started, then his expression darkened.

"Oh, yeah. That's right." He didn't say anything more.

"We can still do something fun," Holly said, determined now to change the mood. "Let's figure out what before you guys go to bed tonight. If we get the paper and see what the weather is supposed to be like tomorrow, we can plan ahead."

Even Aidan, who'd been silent and grumpy, brightened up at that. "Cool. Maybe we can go to the park. Do you think so?"

"It depends on the weather, Aidan. But we'll try."

"All right." It was the first smile she'd seen from him since Alex had left.

"I've got chocolate chip cookies I just baked Sunday. Aidan, you get the glasses, Conor, you get the milk and I'll get the cookies." They weren't the cure for everything, Holly thought, but at least chocolate chip cookies could be a start.

Wednesday dawning sunny felt like another start. Since there was no rush to get to school, or anywhere else, Holly fixed pancakes, usually a Saturday-morning treat. The boys ate well, and got dressed quickly. While she was getting ready herself, Holly had a thought.

She called Felicity, who picked up the phone on the second ring. "What are you doing with Jasmine today? I figure if I'm not working, you're probably picking up the slack. We're going to the park. Want us to pick her up?''

"No, I'll meet you at the park. That way I can run a couple errands before I show up at work. Let me get her ready and pack her a backpack or something in case she gets wet or cruddy or anything outside. See you soon?''

"About half an hour. Meet you at the gazebo?'' Holly hung up, glad to give the boys somebody to play with, and give her friend a break at the same time.

There was a brisk breeze at the park. Holly was glad the boys were both wearing their parkas, and she had remembered her gloves. They had been at the park about ten minutes when Holly saw Felicity and Jasmine drive up.

"Brrr,'' Felicity said, hurrying to the gazebo. "I'm glad it's you out here and not me.''

"It feels good. Bracing.'' They both laughed as they watched the kids run around the playground. Soon there was a game of tag going on over and around the playground equipment. Holly's heart felt lighter than it had in days.

"Don't stay out here longer than you want to, okay?'' Felicity gave her a long look. "You doing all right?''

"I think I am. I'm still a little sore from what

happened Friday, and I have to admit I miss Alex. But I think we're going to be all right.''

"Good. See you about two back at your place, okay?''

"Okay. Say hi to Jon-Paul for me.''

Felicity nodded and headed to her car while Holly watched the children, listening to them when they darted between the pines and she'd lose track of one of them for a moment or two. Jasmine darted out from between two trees onto the wood-chip surface of the playground. Something tripped her up and, shrieking, she fell.

Holly was there as quickly as she could cross the ground between them. Jasmine was already picking herself up, but she was crying. "Ouch," Holly said. "Was it a bad fall? Let's look at you.''

She finished picking Jasmine up, and brushed the front of her off. There were no rips or tears in her jacket or her overalls. "Where does it hurt the most?''

"My hands. And this knee," Jasmine said between hiccuping sobs, pointing to her right leg.

"Lucky you were wearing good mittens, huh? No scrapes, at least. Should we look at that knee?''

Jasmine shook her head. "It's okay. I don't think I need a Band-Aid or anything. Maybe when we go home.''

"Okay." Holly realized that neither boy had run

up to them to see if Jasmine was all right. In fact, it was surprisingly quiet around them.

Holly looked around trying to hear footsteps or voices. There was nothing. "Conor! Aidan! Where are you? This isn't a good time for hide-and-seek."

Across the playground she saw a flash of blue the color of the boys' parkas. "Let's go find them," she told Jasmine, trying not to run or scare the little girl.

Walking as quickly as she could without breaking into a run, she reached the spot where she had seen the blue flash just about the time that Conor leaped out from behind a tree. "Tag, Jasmine. You're it now."

"She fell, Conor. She might not feel like playing right away. Where's your brother?"

Conor's brown eyes looked puzzled. "I don't know, Mom. We're playing tag, remember? He's hiding, I bet."

"Well, the game is over. Aidan! Time to get found now." But no matter how loudly Holly called, Aidan didn't come out from behind any of the trees.

Chapter Fifteen

Fifteen minutes later Holly was hoarse and frantic. It was as if Aidan had vanished. She knew she had to do something, but she wasn't quite sure what to do next. Surely it wasn't a matter for the police, was it? But who else would help her find a little lost boy?

Thanks to the constant reminders Alex had given her, she still had her cell phone, it was charged and right in the driver's-side-door pocket of her car. In less than a minute she was talking to Chief Creasy, who sounded much more serious than she expected him to. "We'll have a couple cars over there in five minutes. Don't go anywhere."

Holly felt almost foolish for causing this much of a stir when Aidan was probably joking around with them. Then she had a thought that made her heart nearly stop. What if this wasn't a joke from Aidan? What if Rico had friends who were out to get revenge? "That can't be possible," she said out loud. "I won't even think about that." But apparently Chief Creasy had, because he and the other officers on duty were at the park in a matter of minutes.

After a little while spent looking around, the chief was shaking his head. "I'm almost sorry for the warmer weather we've had in the past week. It melted the snow, and then dried up the ground. There's not even much of a trail to follow in any direction."

He squatted down in front of Conor. "You wouldn't know anything about this, would you? Your brother say anything to you?"

Conor shook his head. "No, sir. We were just playing tag. Then Jasmine fell down. Then Aidan was gone." His lower lip started trembling.

Holly scooped him up and hugged him tightly, then he slithered out of her arms to stand on the ground. "We'll find him, Conor, don't worry." Wind blew a lock of her hair across her face, and Holly pushed it away. As she did, something else caught her eye. "Tell me I didn't just see snow."

The chief was solemn. "I'd like to pretend I didn't see any, either. But we did, Mrs. Douglas. And we need to get more people out here and start

looking hard for that little boy.'' Holly willed herself not to cry. It wouldn't help find Aidan and it
would only panic Conor and Jasmine. But she certainly wanted to cry right now.

Before she could give in to her feelings, there was
a hand on her shoulder. She turned to see Constance
Laughlin. Constance hugged her as she'd hugged
her little boy, and Holly found it hard not to dissolve
into tears. ''I came as soon as Charles had the dis-
patcher call me. You and I will go to the church,
Holly. We need to let them know what's going on,
and we need to go down to the kitchen and get the
biggest coffeepot going, and some soup. With
weather like this, we'll need to keep everyone ro-
tated through a building to get dried off and warmed
up. First Peninsula is the closest big gathering
place.''

Constance shepherded Holly toward her car,
along with the children. ''Come on and let's get
started. It will keep you busy until they find that
boy.'' Holly was eager to do something, anything
that felt like progress. The sooner Aidan was back
in her arms where she could hold him, the better.

''Constance, you're a marvel.'' Holly didn't know
if she'd ever seen anyone do so much in an hour.
They were in the big gathering room in the lower
level of First Peninsula Church, and it was a hub of

activity. Charles Creasy was already briefing people in one corner, getting them ready to send out on a search effort. And Constance, Elizabeth and Holly were working in the kitchen.

Constance's answering smile was wry. "I wish I'd never learned how to do any of this. If there were no need to organize in times of trouble like this, no one would be good at it. For my part, it's what I can do. I look at it as sort of my ministry."

In the corner, Chief Creasy's volunteers were packing up to head out. Each group had radios for communication and plenty of heavy-weather gear. Surely they would find Aidan quickly.

About five minutes after the searchers left, Wendy got to the church hall, with her preschoolers in tow. "I can't do all that much to help, but I figured I could set up an informal child care in the nursery," she said. "That way you won't worry about Conor or Felicity's little girl, and if anybody wants to join the search efforts or the kitchen crew, they've got someplace to leave their children."

Holly couldn't believe how blessed she felt today. She was still worried and scared about her son, but God was reaching out to her with so many pairs of hands to show how much He cared for her. She hugged Wendy, who hugged her back tightly for a moment, then started her promised task of arranging activities for the children.

"I can't believe I missed the first wave of troops," Reverend Burns said when he came down the stairs to a nearly empty room a few moments later. "Guess I'll have to go get my coat on and head for the park. I'm not letting the searchers all go off without at least a prayer for them and your little boy."

A few more people trickled into the hall in the next half hour, waiting to hear whether a second party of searchers would be needed. Holly was handing out mugs of coffee and setting out a plate of cookies someone had thoughtfully brought with them when she heard sounds that nearly stopped her heart.

The distinctive wail of an ambulance sounded, first in the distance, then louder as it went from the station near the hospital down the main streets of town. Then it became more faint again in the opposite direction, toward the park. Constance recognized it, too, and came over to put an arm around Holly. "It might not be a bad thing. We'll just have to keep praying. We'll hear soon."

They heard more quickly than they expected. Wendy came out of the nursery trailing all her charges and crossed over to the kitchen. "Robert just called me on my cell phone. He knew we would have heard the ambulance and wanted to tell us what was happening." There were tears in her eyes, and Holly's heart was racing so that she had to sit down.

"It's not Aidan," Wendy said, seeing her distress. "It was Reverend Burns."

"Oh, no!" Elizabeth cried in dismay. "What happened? It wasn't his heart?"

"No, thankfully, nothing like that. He took a fall on the ice and did something to his bad knee. Robert insisted he go straight to the hospital, and he said they're likely to transfer him to Green Bay if the fall did as much damage as he suspects it did."

"I feel awful. He did this for my sake, and look what's happened," Holly said, burying her face in her hands. What did she do now? Aidan was still out there, who knew where. They were all doing what they could, everyone was praying non-stop and still things weren't going well at all. What else was there to do?

Conor was climbing up on her lap, pulling her hands away. "Don't cry, Mom. Aidan will get found. I know he will. We should call Alex, Mom. Alex could find him, I bet."

Looking into her son's earnest face, Holly realized he was right. "I bet he could, Conor. Wendy, let me borrow your phone, will you?"

"With pleasure." Wendy handed her the phone and Holly thought for a minute. Alex's own cell phone number came to her mind in a flash and she dialed it.

As it rang she murmured to the ringing phone. "Come on, answer this. Don't be in court already. Don't be—"

"Alex Wilkins." A deep familiar voice broke in to her urgings.

"Hi. It's Holly."

"What's up? Miss me already? You don't sound so good."

"I'm not. I need you. Come back now. I'm not even going to ask if it's convenient or if you would do it, or anything. I never thought I'd say this, Alex, but you're the only one who can help me and I need you here as soon as you can get back to Safe Harbor."

He didn't say no. He didn't say anything right away except for two words. "What's wrong?"

Holly told him, and in his answer were the sweetest words she'd heard all day. "I'm on my way. I'm in a suit, getting ready for court, but I've got other clothes in the car. And thankfully a nearly full tank of gas. It's still two hours driving even if I push."

"Then push, but be careful, too, Alex. I can't imagine what I'd do if something happened to you, too."

"Nothing's happened to Aidan, Holly." He

sounded as if he was trying to reassure himself as much as anything. ''He's just a little bit lost. We'll find him and he'll be back in your arms before dinnertime.''

''I believe you,'' Holly said. *And I love you for saying it,* she wanted to add. But that part she kept in her heart for now as she hung up the phone and began to pray, again, for Aidan's safety and now for Alex, as well.

What was the kid thinking? Alex kept wondering all the way up through Illinois and then Wisconsin, racing as fast as he could in a vehicle without lights and a siren. Fortunately he either looked like a man on a mission or something was shielding him from radar, because no one stopped him during his flying trip.

He broke all his own personal records for travel of that distance, getting to Safe Harbor even more quickly than he'd promised Holly. He made a quick stop at First Peninsula to tell her that he was in town.

The church basement was full of people. Men and women who had obviously been out searching were bent over mugs of coffee and bowls of soup, trying to thaw out. Charles Creasy got up from the end of a table of searchers and shook his hand. He looked kind of worn out, but then given what the man had already had to deal with today, that was understandable. "I'm glad to see you. We've drawn a blank so far." Alex wasn't quite sure how his coming would change that, but he'd do everything he could.

"Let me tell Holly I'm here, and I'll get ready to head out."

"Great. I think she's back in the kitchen with some of the other women."

Alex found her sitting on a high stool, scraping carrots from a large bag. He suspected someone had given her the task to keep her mind occupied, and he thought it was a great idea. She was still turned halfway toward the door, so that motion into the room would catch her eye, and she dropped the carrot and the peeler the moment she saw him. "Oh, am I glad to see you," she said, coming into his arms in a satisfying, solid way. She felt slight gathered in there, which Alex knew was deceptive. Here was a woman made of steel under a velvet exterior.

"Yeah, well, it could be better circumstances and all that, but I'm glad you called," he told her, putting his head down to nuzzle the fantastic fragrance of her hair before letting her go so they could talk.

"I just came back here to tell you I'd made it, and I'm heading out to the park. Anything else I should know?"

"Not really. I keep thinking it's something you know already that's going to make the difference in finding him. I don't know what it is, but I just feel that way. Conor swears Aidan didn't say anything unusual this morning. He was very glad we were going to the park when I told him last night. What was going on, Alex?'' Her violet eyes clouded with worry.

Alex had been searching his thoughts for hours now trying to come up with the key to Aidan's disappearance. He hated to tell Holly that he agreed that it had something to do with his own leaving town. But what? Was he just running away to get attention? Was there more to it than that?

''Aidan's not much of a talker.'' He knew that wasn't telling Holly anything, but it did help Alex organize his thoughts. ''I tried to explain why I was leaving to him, but I feel like I did a lousy job. Even the last time, when we were on the way to school Monday morning, I never felt like I got down to his level.''

''Did you say anything different then?''

''Not really. I just tried to make him understand that I had a job to go back to do, and I had promised to do it. Gave him the usual adult reasons for why his opinion didn't matter, I guess, and why I was going to do something else instead.'' Even as Alex said that, he had a growing hunch where to look for Aidan Douglas. Because when he replayed their conversation in his head, and tried to listen to it from a five-year-old's literal perspective, suddenly he knew.

"What?" Holly could sense the difference in him.

He smiled down at her questioning gaze. "You. Talking to you made all the difference." He kissed her full on the mouth, for inspiration and to seal the promise he was about to make. "I'll be back with him. Soon." Holly was probably a little surprised by all that, but Alex didn't look back to see. He knew where to find Aidan now—at least he thought he did—and it was time to go do it.

The wind out on the nature trails that led higher into the park was wicked. It was spitting sleet now and the light was getting dimmer as the afternoon faded. Alex knew they didn't have much more than an hour or two before it got dark and they'd have to call off the search until morning. That would be worrisome, even though Aidan was healthy and had warm clothes on.

He'd told Charles his idea, and as a result about half a dozen of the chief's most rested searchers had headed out. When the trails branched off as they went higher into the hills above town, they had split up. Alex was following a little-used part of one of the trails that led high into the hills. It didn't look welcoming, but he didn't think Aidan would have thought about that. He was a kid with a mission, and this trail fit the bill.

Alex thought back to Monday, wishing he could have an instant replay of their conversation. He'd been around Holly's boys long enough by now to know how literal they were. Why had he told a kindergartner that he had to take the high ground on something? Sure, an adult would see that as a figure of speech. But not a kid like Aidan. So now Alex was pretty sure that he'd taken the first chance he got to head for the highest spot he could think of. It was touching that he meant that much to the boy, that he would go look for him this way. Maybe that thought would even keep him from hollering at the kid for scaring his mother and everybody in town, once Alex found him.

The brush was pretty thick up here, and the ice and sleet didn't make travel any easier. Past a curve in the trail Alex could see a clearing ahead where the brush thinned into an open spot. There was a rocky wall of ledge jutting out into the clearing, forming a natural shelter, and there Alex could see two figures huddled at a small fire near the rock wall. ''Aidan,'' he called, and the smaller figure turned in his direction.

''Alex? That you? Have you been up here all the time?''

''No, I've been in Chicago, like I told you,'' he said, crossing the icy clearing. ''I came back to help look for you.''

"I kind of got lost. I was looking for you, and you found me, so I guess that's okay." The boy turned to the man beside the fire. "This is Mr. Nathan. He says we're going down the mountain once I get warm."

The man stuck out a gloved hand to Alex. "Nathan Taylor. He looked a little worse for wear, so I got the fire going for a while. I figured once this let up a little we'd head down."

"How long ago did you find him?"

"Long enough to get the fire going. I used to be from around here, and I came up here earlier today to get a good view of things. You can see the whole town from the other side of this ridge." He motioned past the ledge. "Once the weather turned, I decided to wait it out before sliding down the trails to town. Then Aidan here happened by, and now you."

Taylor seemed like an honest soul. Of course, Alex knew that plenty of the people he dealt with in life could look honest when they had to, but there seemed to be a quality about this man's piercing blue eyes and forthright demeanor that made Alex trust him. And he'd done the right thing by Aidan, so Alex had to admit he didn't really care what his business was otherwise. "Well, we better get him down this hill and back to his mom before she totally loses it," Alex told him. "I sure appreciate your trouble. You can probably get a hero's welcome if you come down to First Peninsula Church with me.''

Taylor shook his head. "Thanks, but I'd rather not. I've got unfinished business in Safe Harbor, and I haven't figured out just where the Lord is leading me in relation to the town, and some folks in it, yet.'' He gave Alex a long look. "I'd appreciate if you left my part in this out of the telling where you could.''

"I'll try. But your new friend is five, and kids say just about anything. And I'll definitely have to tell his mother.''

"I understand. But for general consumption I'd appreciate you just saying a hiker found him on the trails, and he's a shy individual when it comes to attention.''

"I can do that.'' For many men Alex wouldn't hedge on the truth like that, but he just had the feeling it was the right thing to do with Nathan Taylor. He looked down at Aidan. "Come on, buddy, let's get you back to your mom.''

Aidan sighed. "I'm in trouble, aren't I?''

Alex wasn't going to skirt the truth for Aidan. "Yeah, you are. But I have a feeling that your mom will be so glad to see you that she'll forget about that part for at least half an hour. After that you'll probably have a lecture to listen to. And let me be the first to tell you that you deserve it.''

Aidan sighed again. "Let's get it over with, then." He squared his shoulders and looked back at Nathan. "Thanks for the fire, mister. Will I see you again?"

"Probably so, son. Now go find your mother." And with that Aidan took Alex's hand and he led the boy down the trail to where he radioed the other searchers that their job was done.

Chapter Sixteen

"I have to go back, you know." It was the first thing Alex had said to her after he'd put Aidan into her arms.

"I know," she told him, not letting go of her squirmy son despite his protests that he was much too big for all this squeezing. "I didn't expect you to stay."

"Didn't you? Then why did you call me?" Alex looked confused.

"Because it was the right thing to do. Because I knew that I needed you, and I had to tell you just that. There's more to it than that, Alex. I not only need you, I love you. Both of those things are hard for me to admit." She finally gave up and let Aidan slide to the floor. Giving him a stern look, she directed him to the stool next to her and handed him a cookie and a mug of cocoa that Constance had ladled for him. "And you, young man, don't you dare go anyplace else. Understand?" He nodded, wide-eyed, and sat still, not even picking up his cookie for a moment.

"Wow. Alex said I'd be in trouble. He was right."

"Yes, he was. Alex has been right about most things since we got to know him. That's one of the reasons I love him. And he's right now when he says he has to go back to Chicago, Aidan, so don't go off anywhere looking for him again once he's gone, understand?"

Aidan sighed and picked up his cocoa. "I guess."

"He doesn't have to go looking for me, Holly. That's what I'm trying to tell you." Alex had taken off his gloves, and he used one index finger to tilt her chin up so that she was looking straight into his eyes. "I have to go back. But not for long."

"No?" Holly's mouth was suddenly so dry that she couldn't say anything else.

"No. I have a court appearance I can't foist off on anybody else. I got a continuance today to come find Aidan, but I have to deal with this case. It's tying up the loose ends with Salazar and the others involved with him. And it's the last thing I'm doing for Cook County. I've already given them two weeks' notice.''

Holly's heart was beating so fast that she could hardly stand it. Alex's fingertips were still caressing her chin, and she couldn't push them away. Looking up into his eyes seemed like just the right thing to do. ''And then what happens?''

''Then I move to Safe Harbor, Wisconsin, and see about finding space for a decent family law practice, something I'm told the town lacks. And I intend to buy a house over in Harbor Hills that's big enough for a family eventually, and see if I can convince a certain stubborn widow that she needs to come live there. Eventually. After I court her and marry her. On her own time, of course.''

''Oh. I have a feeling she can be convinced,'' Holly told him as his arms came around her. ''She's not as stubborn as she used to be.''

''Mom?'' Aidan broke in to her thoughts. ''Hey, Mom? Can I move now? I need to get down.''

''What for, Aidan?'' She hated to break this wonderful moment when for a change everything in her life seemed just right.

''I spilled my cocoa and my lap's getting all wet. And sticky.''

''Then get down and ask Mrs. Laughlin for a towel, Aidan.'' With this many friends surrounding her, Holly figured that maybe just once one of them could handle a crisis.

"You're not more mad at me?" He sounded surprised.

"Not this time. Accidents happen. Right, Alex?"

"Right. And we don't need anybody crying over spilt milk. Or cocoa," he murmured, pulling her even deeper into an embrace. "So you think I have a chance?"

"More than a chance," she told him, snuggling into his embrace. "I think this is a new beginning to a wonderful life for all of us." And there in the harbor of his arms, she believed every word.

"I hear this is a party to open more than one business," Annie Simmons said as Holly and Alex came into the Lighthouse Bed-and-Breakfast on Saturday night. Alex had made it back to Safe Harbor in time to have dinner with the family on Friday night and spend the weekend. Holly knew he'd still be shuttling back and forth to Chicago for two more weeks, but it was wonderful to have him in town even for the weekends.

"Well, that may be a little premature," Alex told her. "I still haven't hung out my shingle yet. But Wilkins Family Law will be a reality in Safe Harbor as soon as it's feasible. I'm hoping by Memorial Day we can be up and running."

"Great. Are you going to work for him?" Annie asked Holly as she took her coat and added it to the growing number on the coatrack.

"Not right away. Jon-Paul would have a fit. Besides, I know almost nothing about legal practice."

"You can always learn," Alex said, putting an arm around her. He looked happy and relaxed in this party setting. "I'd love having you around all the time."

"You're so sweet to say that, but you've never seen me type. For right now I'll be better off staying at The Bistro. Maybe I can convince Jon-Paul to move me permanently to lunch shift so we can have evenings together anyway. Would you like that?"

"I'd love it. Not as much as I love you, but having every evening together would be a great start. We could have romantic macaroni-and-cheese dinners with the boys and all do the dishes together," he said. The gleam in his eye told Holly he was only half teasing.

"Well, we'll discuss it later. Right now we have a party to attend, Mr. Wilkins." She grasped the hand that encircled her waist and pulled him into the breakfast room, where people were nibbling snacks, visiting and enjoying the view out of the bank of windows that faced the lake. Even in the dark the lights of houses and boats far along the shore made for a spectacular sight.

"Hey, look who's back in town already," Wendy called. She and Robert were in one corner, balancing soft drinks and snacks and chatting with Elizabeth. "Are you back to stay, Alex?"

"Just weekends for a little while longer," he said as they moved over to the doctor and his wife.

"We can hardly wait to have you as a permanent resident of the town," Wendy said. "And I'm sure Chief Creasy will be glad to have another possible recruit around."

"No, I'm leaving that part of my career behind for good. I want to keep things as safe as possible around me to convince Holly I'm a good risk for marriage. In fact, if you have any leads on where I could find office space for a family law practice, I'd be obliged."

Robert Maguire smiled. "I might at that. I think last month at the Rotary meeting the president of Harbor Federal said something about one of the office suites in his building. Call me Monday and I'll put you in touch with him."

"Thanks. And now let's talk about something besides business, since this is a party. How do you like the paint job on the trim in here? I can claim responsibility for at least half of it." Holly enjoyed the broad grin Alex had on his face. "This is why I want to practice law instead of going into the remodeling business."

"Hey, it looks great. Annie's done so much with this building."

"Yes, and she already has her first customer." Wendy motioned across the room to where a middle-aged man stood with his back to them. "His name is Nathan Taylor, and he says he plans on spending weekends here often."

Holly looked over at the man, wondering if he could be the mysterious Nathan who'd had a hand in rescuing Aidan. She arched a brow in what she hoped was a silent question to Alex, who nodded slightly. "Excuse us while we go welcome him to town," Alex said smoothly, guiding her toward Nathan Taylor.

"Thanks for keeping things to yourself," he said softly as they crossed the room. "I don't think Aidan's rescuer cares much for publicity."

When they joined him Nathan was standing by the fireside, appearing to be lost in thought. "Mr. Taylor? I'm Holly Douglas. Aidan's mother." Holly found she couldn't say anything else because of a lump in her throat.

"Hello. It's nice to meet you." Nathan Taylor had the keenest blue eyes she'd ever seen. Alex had told her that there was something deeply trustworthy about the man, and now Holly could see for herself why he'd said that. "I hope you haven't said much to anybody. I couldn't help but overhear Alex, and he's right. I'm not much for publicity, and I'm really enjoying Safe Harbor. How's my young friend doing? No more serious trouble?''

"Nothing besides the normal scrapes a five-year-old boy gets into, thankfully. He told me all about you, but he understands that you'd rather not have the world know about your rescue effort, and I've kept things quiet, as well.''

Taylor's face relaxed. "Good. In God's own good time I may have plenty to say to folks in this town. But for now I'd just as soon stay in the background like this. In fact, I may retire to my room and let the locals enjoy the party." He excused himself and crossed the busy room.

As he was walking out, Constance Laughlin and Charles Creasy were arriving, and Nathan and Constance found themselves face-to-face for a moment. Holly was too far away to see what passed between them. But she noticed that afterward her friend had a strange look on her face.

"Who is that man?" Constance asked when she saw Holly a moment later.

"His name is Nathan Taylor. He's Annie's first guest here at the bed-and-breakfast.''

"Do you know him?" Annie asked.

Constance looked flushed and slightly disturbed. "No, I don't think so. But there's something so familiar about him. If I believed in the notion of past lives, which I don't, I'd almost say…'' Then she trailed off and waved her hand. "But that's ridiculous."

Chief Creasy came over then and put a solicitous hand on Constance's shoulder. "You look warm. Want to move away from the fire and get a cup of punch? We might let these two have a little privacy, since Alex is only here for a couple days before he goes back to the city again."

Alex laughed, and Holly reveled in the sound of it. "She'll get plenty tired of my company before long, Charles. I'd rather socialize tonight and get to know my new neighbors. Let's go find that punch and you can tell me about the business climate in Safe Harbor."

"It's growing and changing, I can tell you that. We've got a couple new places opening up on Market Square, always a good sign. Let's get Constance a cold drink and I'll tell you more."

The four of them crossed the room again to where the buffet was laid out. Holly didn't realize until she got there that she was holding Alex's hand as if it were the most natural thing in the world. It was a perfect night and another new beginning, she reflected. She had so much to be thankful for. Impulsively she leaned over and kissed Alex on the cheek.

"What was that for?" he asked, smiling.

"Nothing in particular. And everything." She

smiled back, knowing that he would understand. She could depend on him for that, and for so much more. Here among the friends that meant as much as family, Holly could hardly wait to see how this new chapter of her life began.

* * * * *

Be sure to watch for Annie's story,
INNER HARBOR,
coming only to
Love Inspired in April 2003.

And now for a sneak preview,
please turn the page.

Chapter One

"Since you're going to be living here, I wonder if you'd be interested in playing for our children's choir—the same music you played today. Easter morning." Annie rushed on, blurting out the facts in no particular order. "They're good kids, but I can't direct and play, and they need to practice and memorize their parts. We haven't yet begun to coordinate with the readers and that will take a lot of work to get the timing right, and—"

"Okay."

"And then of course, there are the robes to think of. Someone else is handling them, but I expect—" She stopped, stared at him. "What did you say?"

"I said I'll play for you. The organ?" Russ's eyes sparkled with mirth. "That was what you asked, wasn't it?"

"Oh. Yes, it was." Annie gulped. That easy? "Thank you."

"You're welcome." He licked the white Danish icing off his fingertips, then took a sip of coffee before tilting back in his chair like a satisfied cat just finishing a bowl of cream. "Actually, I wanted to talk to you about something else."

"Talk to *me?*" she demanded, suspicious of the odd smile twitching at his handsome mouth. "Why?"

"Calm down. It's nothing horrible," Russ assured her. "I can see the worst ideas flickering through your eyes."

"What could you possibly have to talk to me about? We've only just met."

"Remember I told you we used to come here in the summer?"

She nodded.

"My parents are both lawyers in Chicago. They're very busy. Back then they lived in Green Bay and they wanted a place nearby where our family could get away from work and relax together." His voice tightened a fraction.

"Oh, yes." She still didn't see what that had to do with her.

"My grandparents would come sometimes, too. My grandfather wasn't crazy about leaving work. He was a workaholic, and lazing around made him very uncomfortable. But my mom loved having her mother visit us at the cottage and my gran adored the lake. They spent a lot of time talking. My grandfather didn't dare put a damper on that, because Gran was the love of his life." Those unusual eyes darkened with emotion. "Their marriage was perfect, exactly what everyone thinks of when they say the word *love*."

"Oh." Where was this going? "They were your only grandparents?"

"The only ones I knew. Dad's parents died before I was born. They lived in New York."

Mitchard. The name pricked her memory. A newspaper article, what, a month ago? Something named in memory, wasn't it? Annie stared at him. "The land developer?"

He smiled. "Uh-huh."

"Oh." What else was there to say? Russ Mitchard's grandfather had been a household name and certainly a workaholic. No wonder he hadn't wanted to put grandiose building schemes aside to traipse around Door County. If she remembered correctly, the son, Russ's father, was an only child, and had inherited everything when the senior Mitchard had a heart attack. Curiosity got the better of her.

"With that history, it seems strange you'd choose

the career you have. I'd have thought you'd follow your grandfather, build more office buildings.''

''There's nothing wrong with what I do.''

The belligerent words startled her.

''I didn't say there was. I just thought—'' She stopped when his face darkened. ''Never mind.'' She sipped her coffee, thinking. ''So you came back to Safe Harbor because of your memories.''

''I came back because the marketing studies I commissioned showed great potential for my business here.'' The words stopped abruptly.

''Good for you. And welcome to our town.'' She tried to lighten the tone.

''I have another reason for staying, though, Annie.'' He peered at her.

''Really?'' She laughed nervously. There was something about those unusual eyes. ''Well, according to the Chamber of Commerce there are a lot of reasons anyone would choose Safe Harbor.''

''It had nothing to do with the Chamber of Commerce. I'd already decided to set up shop here, just not quite yet. But then my grandfather upped the ante. More particularly, his will did.''

Something—a fizzle of awareness—shot through her. ''Your grandfather's will said you had to live in Safe Harbor?'' she whispered.

''No.'' He took a deep breath and looked her straight in the eye. ''My grandfather's will said I have to marry you to collect my inheritance.''

Dear Reader,

For authors, every book written teaches us something as well as lets us tell a story. Some of the material in *The Harbor of His Arms* is quite personal for me. Like Holly, I have had times when I have struggled to resolve how the life of a faithful Christian can be touched by things like clinical depression. For anyone who thinks they might be walking that same path, let me reassure you that God is our constant companion in any time of trouble, and He provides so many ways out of the depths of our despair.

Personally, my life is filled with much more joy than despair most of the time. If you read the dedication, you'll see that, as always, I've dedicated the book first to my dear husband. For this one he doesn't have to share the dedication with anyone else, as he usually does. I figure every twenty-five years or so, a guy should get something to himself.

Blessings,

Lynn Bulock

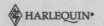

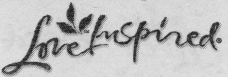